FLOSSED IN LOVE

ANGELA PEARSE

© 2025 by Angela Pearse

The moral right of the author has been asserted.
All rights reserved.
No part of this book may be reproduced or used in any manner without written permission of the copyright owner.
First paperback edition June 2025.
Published by Clamp Ltd. (clamp.pub)

Set in Mick Caster and Sabon.
Cover art by My Lan Khuc Valle.

ISBN 978-1-914531-75-0 Paperback (IngramSpark)

Author Note

Chapter 1

Florence | Edinburgh, present day

The blood-curdling scream is so loud it makes my molars tingle. I've been slouching in a plastic bucket chair, but my spine straightens at the noise, half expecting the receptionist to sprint down the corridor and exclaim, 'What the hell was that?'

As to what's taking place behind the door, I have no ready answer. Murder most foul? I've heard a lot of screams in my life, and that one sounded particularly painful.

When no one comes running, I figure the receptionist mustn't be bothered, or she's gone home. Either way, I'm trapped out here listening to whatever's going on in there. Another ragged screech makes me almost jump out of my skin. It trails off into a bubbling gurgle.

Jesus!

I'm starting to think my clever idea of booking the last appointment of the day to get my teeth checked wasn't so clever after all. Maybe I should ...

I rise from the chair with the intention of legging it, but

the exam room door swings open. A man stumbles out, clutching his unshaven cheek, surrounded by a miasma of stale alcohol. 'Good luck, you'll need it,' he mutters and staggers off down the corridor.

'Florence Hughes? I'm ready for you now,' a gravelly male voice intones from inside the room.

That's odd. I've been coming to this private dental practice for years. My dentist, Dr Heather Malcolm, is a lovely middle-aged woman with a gentle touch whom I like chatting to. Unless she's had a voice transplant, this isn't her. Has she taken on a colleague? If so, he sounds like he might be a sadist!

As I'm standing there, deliberating, a tall guy with broad shoulders appears in the doorway, he's wearing a white coat and a blue surgical mask. His short hair is coffee-coloured with several streaks of vivid purple. *An edgy young dentist, that's a first. Though it was Halloween last week, so perhaps he went to a party ...*

'Are you Florence Hughes?' the guy enquires, his voice muffled by the mask.

I nod, but my eyes zero in on his white coat. There's a smear of blood on one lapel, and I can smell it. It's been several days since I've had a drink, and the tantalising tangy scent teases my nose, making it difficult to concentrate.

'Yes ... yes, I am,' I manage to get out.

'Please come in. Sorry to have kept you waiting.' He steps aside, and I enter the room, pinching my nostrils shut with two fingers as I pass by so I don't smell the blood. I've worked hard over the years to master my self-control, but still ...

He gestures to the dentist chair and says, 'Take a seat. I'll be with you in just a minute.' His accent isn't Scottish; it's got a distinctly English clipped-vowel ring to it. My curiosity is piqued. I'm a sucker for a well-spoken Englishman. Don't get me wrong—guys with Scottish accents are hot too, but only if you can understand them.

Dutifully, I hop up onto the blue vinyl chair and stretch out my legs, wondering what he was doing to his previous patient to make him scream like that. There's no evidence of a struggle, and the small sink next to me is clean, though I can detect remnants of blood-infused spittle. My gums start prickling, and I press my lips together tightly, willing my fangs not to extend. *Dammit, I should have had a mouthful at least before I came out.* But our blood supply is running low, so I was being altruistic.

What's this sadist dentist doing? He's taking ages. Impatiently, I swivel my head and see him checking my previous X-rays on his computer—closely.

I whip back around as he rolls up next to me in his chair. He clips a paper towel around my neck.

'So I'll just do a routine check-up today. Your X-rays are good until your next visit—'

I interrupt his dentist spiel. 'Where's Dr Malcolm? I usually see her.'

His eyebrows lift slightly. 'Dr Malcolm retired six months ago, I'm afraid.'

'Retired?' I repeat, a bit shocked and disappointed as I really did like her; she never asked awkward questions, and she reminded me of my Aunt Ivy. But she must've been older than she looked. Come to think of it, she did mention something about retiring last time I saw her ...

'I'm Dr Damian Rhodes. Hopefully, I'm a suitable replacement?' The corners of his greeny-hazel eyes crinkle as if he's smiling underneath his mask, and I sense that he's trying to put me at ease. They probably have an entire semester dedicated to chairside manner at dental school— and how to deal with people screaming blue murder. He doesn't seem too rattled about that.

'I'm fine with it, but I'm not sure your previous patient was,' I say, attempting a joke.

'Ah, yes, sorry you had to hear that. He needed a tooth pulled and didn't want anaesthetic. He insisted that he'd taken enough whisky to numb the pain. Newsflash: he hadn't. Things got a bit ... messy.'

'So I see,' I say, staring pointedly at his bloody lapel.

His eyes follow the direction of my gaze. 'Damn, sorry. Normally, my assistant would be here to point out things like that, but she's off sick today. I think I have a spare coat. I'll change ...'

He starts to get up, and I sigh inwardly. 'It's fine. Honestly, I just want to get this over with ... I mean, it's not a problem.'

'OK, if you don't mind. Thanks.' Dr Rhodes lowers the chair until I'm flat on my back and at his mercy. He yanks his tray of dental implements closer with a rattle and selects one. 'Not a fan of going to the dentist, Florence?' he asks conversationally. 'Open wide for me.'

I grunt in reply and open my mouth as wide as I can. Dr Rhodes pokes around my gumline methodically with a pointy-ended instrument, inserting it between my teeth. He does some further checks with another instrument. Finishing those, he presses around my jaw and rubs a gloved finger up under my gums, and my stomach muscles tense—he's worryingly thorough.

His index finger brushes against my eye teeth, and I stiffen. My fangs only fully extend when summoned by bloodlust, and they don't show on my X-rays so I should be OK. But the dentist feels the pointy tips and says, 'These are a bit sharp. I could file them for you if it's an issue?'

I shake my head and he doesn't comment further. I relax

after that, relieved that he hasn't noticed anything too out of the ordinary about me.

'Well, I'm happy to say your teeth are pristine, Florence,' he remarks, sounding bemused. 'You don't have any fillings, and there isn't even any tartar to scrape off. What's your secret?'

He moves slightly and I get another whiff of the blood on his lapel.

'I don't eat sugar,' I say tightly, my nostrils flaring. *God, I'm going to suck that blood bag dry when I get home. Altruism be damned.*

'Do you floss regularly?'

I nod. 'Yes.' It's true, I do because sometimes blood clots catch in my teeth. It's one of the drawbacks of drinking under-the-table transfusions. But probably best not to mention that ...

'What about TePe brushes?'

I shake my head.

Then ensues a rather long lecture about the benefits of using TePe dental brushes, and he thrusts several different-sized ones between my teeth. I'm given a couple of blue TePe brushes and a tiny tube of toothpaste in a small baggie. Woo-hoo, free dental merch. Bonus.

If my flatmates, Sadie and Hester, could hear this conversation, they'd laugh their heads off. Luckily, I'm out of range, so neither of them can. I know what Sadie would say too as she doesn't have a filter: 'You weirdo, why are you bothering when you don't actually need to go to the dentist?' Perhaps it is a bit strange; after all, I never have to worry about tooth decay even if I don't brush. But is it so wrong to want to feel like I'm part of society every once in a while? And since Dr Malcolm's replacement is a young (possibly handsome) dentist, at least I'm good in the sexual fantasy department for the next year. Men in masks have a certain je ne sais quoi, and I have a vivid imagination.

The chair is slowly uprighted to its original position, and Dr Rhodes tells me he's finished. I sit there, unmoving, as a deep well of disappointment opens up inside me. So soon? Can we not chat some more about TePe brushes? Maybe I should say I'm thinking of becoming a dental hygienist, and does he have any career advice?

But I don't want him to think I'm a lonely saddo.

'Great, thank you,' I say brightly, self-preservation overriding my need for human connection, as it always does.

Dr Rhodes switches off the light above my head and idly removes his surgical mask. I sit there for a moment as the sight of him sinks in. He's ridiculously hot for a human; as well as those lovely greeny-hazel eyes, he has a straight nose and a strong jaw.

He smiles at me in a professional manner and his teeth are, of course, outstanding. A playful dimple appears in his left cheek and my stomach flips. It's the cherry on top of a gorgeous man sundae. Peeling off his gloves with a snap, he drops them on the tray, and rolls back towards the computer in his chair. 'You're all good to go, Florence. See you next year. Just book an appointment at reception ...'

Dr Rhodes goes through his wrap-up spiel, yadda yadda yadda, but I hardly hear a word he's saying because bloodlust is strumming through my veins. I want to see him again and I don't want to have to wait until next year. Maybe a little vampiric encouragement is all he needs to ask me out?

CHAPTER 2

Florence | London, 1888

My dear deluded Aunt Ivy has arranged this ridiculous appointment for me. She believes I have hidden talents, so much so that she answered a gentleman's advertisement for a governess on my behalf.

Now here I am, staring at a bronze knocker in the shape of a lion's head attached to a glossy black door. My knees tremble as I raise a hand to the ring protruding from the lion's mouth, but I can't quite bring myself to use it.

I've never been in Belgravia before, and the neighbourhood exudes a quiet stately swank. Number 19 South Eaton Place with its creamy white columns is no exception; even the immaculate black-marble stoop is too posh for the likes of me to be standing on it in my tattered boots.

When I found out what Aunt Ivy had done, I was astounded at her gumption. I despise the long hours of my poorly paid sewing work and wish to better myself, as Aunt Ivy well knows. However, I have no wish to make a fool of myself either.

'What on earth possessed you to do such a thing? I have no experience as a governess!'

Aunt Ivy was undeterred. 'You can read and write, and you've always got your nose in a library book. You're perfect for the position. The gentleman is a doctor, and his son is a young boy. *He* won't care if you make a few fumbles. If he asks questions you can't answer, just make something up. You've got a quick tongue in your head. But for the love of God, don't say you're from Spitalfields. Your story is that you're an intelligent, respectable girl being brought up by your aunt, and we live in Kensington. Just remember that at your interview, and you'll be fine.'

'Where exactly is this position?' I demanded.

'Belgravia. He's paying 100 pounds a year, *and* it's live-in. The appointment is at ten o'clock tomorrow.' She clapped her hands excitedly.

'But ... but there will be other women applying who are much more qualified than me. I can't compete—'

'Nonsense, Floss! Of course you can. You have to have more confidence in yourself.'

She'd chivvied and cooed and inflated my head so much that I'd marched out of the door of our damp, shabby flat in London's East End with my chin lifted and my stride purposeful to catch an omnibus. I *felt* good enough, so why shouldn't I apply?

But my best day dress is 6 years old with well-disguised patches (thanks to my careful sewing), and I have a fake reference in my pocket. Unsurprisingly, my false bravado has leaked away like drain water. How on earth will I convince this gentleman—this Dr Alexander Dryden—that I'm better educated than his son, a boy who has been raised in a household infinitely wealthier than my own? It's a ruse that can only end in embarrassment (mine) and laughter (Dr Dryden's). Hot tears edge from my eyes, and I blink them away furiously.

I have two choices: run away and face the wrath of Aunt Ivy *or* knock on the door and face the pity of Dr Dryden. It all boils down to what I'm afraid of the most.

I raise my hand to the lion's ring. Aunt Ivy is terrifying when she's angry.

My tentative rapping is answered by a dark-haired man with a stern expression. 'I have an appointment—with Dr Dryden,' I whisper.

I'm waved inside with a curt 'Follow me.'

At first, I think the man is the butler until I'm ushered into a study, and he enters and closes the door after him. Then I realise this *is* Dr Alexander Dryden, and he doesn't have a butler.

That's slightly odd to my way of thinking, but I suppose

it's not unheard-of.

Dr Dryden seats himself behind the wide wooden desk and gestures to a high-back chair opposite.

'Take a seat, Miss ... ?' His tone is polite, but none too friendly.

I sink into the chair nervously, laying my sweaty palms face down on my thighs.

'Hughes, Florence Hughes.'

'Ah yes.' He ticks something on a piece of paper with a black-and-gold fountain pen. Curiously, I jut my head forward, straining to see how many names are on his list. But his arm covers it.

'Reference?'

Heart pounding, I draw Aunt Ivy's reference out of my pocket and hand over the sealed envelope. Dr Dryden flicks open the flap with a gold letter opener and draws out a single sheet of thin paper. I cringe at the slight twitch of his eyebrow. One page does not bode well. But Aunt Ivy insisted that a short note sticking to the facts—stating where, when, and for whom I had worked—was best. 'If I wax lyrical about your merits, he might get suspicious,' she asserted. But now I'm thinking that she should have tried to fill at least two sheets of thin paper with my merits to give him something more to read.

Dr Dryden peruses the reference in silence. As I know the

gist of what Aunt Ivy has written (and we had a run-through of my answers the night before), I take the chance to observe him, unnoticed.

He's in his early forties and wears his short, straight dark hair in a severe slicked-back style, which draws attention to his pale face, sharp features, and well-trimmed sideburns touched with silver. Dr Dryden is handsome, I conclude, but his personality lacks warmth; in fact, the thing that stands out to me most about him is his decidedly chilly manner. When he raises his unblinking brown eyes from the page to study me, it feels like he's assessing not only my suitability as a governess but also the suitability of my soul for heaven. I lower my gaze in increments under his potent stare until all I'm seeing are my shaking white hands.

The chair creaks as Dr Dryden flexes his legs underneath the desk. Still, he says nothing, but I can sense him inspecting me. It's a kind of mental torture, exacerbated by the hypnotic tick of the clock on the mantel.

My drowsy eyelids start closing—the early start and the haphazard journey across town, which involved three omnibuses, catching up with me.

'Do you eat meat, Miss Hughes?'

Dr Dryden's deep voice cuts through my stupor and jerks me awake.

I blink. 'Pardon?'

'Do. You. Eat. Meat,' he repeats slowly as if I'm hard of hearing.

'Yes, of course,' I say, bewildered. 'Why?'

'Do you like it bloody or well done?'

'Um, well done, I suppose?' *That's a strange question. Why does he want to know that?*

Dr Dryden makes a quick note with his pen. He taps the end of it against his chin and looks at me.

'Where do you really live, Miss Hughes? I've interviewed two young women from Kensington so far, and your dress and manner are far removed from that part of town. And your reference has obviously been faked.'

My chest tightens, and I open my mouth. But I'm not sure what to say, so I close it again. He attempts a smile, but it's a mere parting of his lips, and I catch a brief glimpse of snowy-white teeth.

'I'm not angry. I'm simply curious as to why you'd apply for a position that you're not qualified to do,' he says.

'And I'm curious as to why you're asking me how I like my meat,' I retort. 'Shouldn't you be asking me proper questions, like ... like ...' I trail off as I've never applied for a position like this, and I have no idea what questions he should be asking.

Stupid sodding job. I didn't want it anyway. So what if I would have lived in a fancy house and been paid a decent wage? It's not meant for the likes of me. He's earmarked one of his hoity-toity Kensington girls for it. I let out a doleful sigh. There's no point trying to carry on the pretence, so I may as well come clean. Aunt Ivy is going to be livid that I haven't stuck to my story.

'All right, if you really want to know, I live in Spitalfields with my aunt. She applied to your advertisement and wrote me the reference because she thinks ... Well, never mind what she thinks. But if you'd known my background, you'd never even have given me a chance.'

'Possibly,' he says. 'But lying about who you are doesn't give a good first impression, does it?'

I hang my head, ashamed. 'No, sir. But if it's any consolation, I wasn't entirely comfortable with lying about it.'

'So do you have any experience being a governess? Have you taught any children at all?'

'No. Well, unless you count how to steal a hot potato when the seller's back is turned.'

Dr Dryden lets out a loud bark of laughter. The sound is alarming, but at least he's amused. I smile faintly as he chuckles away.

Speaking of children, where is his son? I wonder. *Upstairs, playing?* Yet from the quick peer down the dimly lit hall before I was shown into his study, I got the impression the house was completely devoid of life. And since I've been in here, there's been no thumps, bumps, or squeals issuing from overhead—no noises that could be associated with a happy young boy playing at least. *Perhaps he's out with his nanny or is just very quiet?*

CHAPTER 3

Damian | Edinburgh, present day

Why on earth did I ask out a patient? What the hell possessed me? I could leave now, and she'll never know I was here.

I'm sitting in a speakeasy cocktail bar but my thoughts are anything but 'easy' about this situation. I've arrived early enough that leaving *is* still a possibility. I take a deep breath to calm my nerves. *Standing her up is a dick move*, I tell myself. *You asked her out, now you have to go through with it.* So I force myself to stay where I am. Part of me is curious to see if Florence shows up, and I haven't been on a date in ages, though I'm not sure what we'll have in common.

For something to do, I flick through the black art deco menu with its eclectic assortment of cocktails while glancing surreptitiously at the entrance every five seconds.

I usually don't have any issue with beautiful girls who lie in my chair with their pearly whites on display. They're patients. Off-limits. I most certainly *never* ask for their phone number at the end of an appointment. But Florence just smiled, shrugged, and typed it into my phone as if it happened to her all the time. Our text conversation that night went off without a hitch. I asked if she was free on Friday. She replied right away, said that she was, and suggested The Brief Encounter, this bar in Stockbridge.

I roll back my shoulders and check if my hair gel is holding.

Just play it cool. Maybe get yourself a drink for something to do. That's an excellent idea.

At the bar, I order a dram of Glenlivet and down it in one. It tastes like caramel fire as it slides down my throat, and my ears start burning, then my chest. But my nerves remain on edge.

'Another please,' I say, and the barman looks amused.

'Hard day at work or a hot date?'

'Both,' I mutter, slinking back to the table, clutching my refill.

I'm three sips in when Florence appears, poised in the doorway, scanning the room. Looking for me.

Holy hell, she's even prettier than I remember.

I have but moments to observe her before she notices me

hidden away here in the back. Her flowing jet-black hair, large violet eyes, and pale skin are a striking combination. The dark-purple lipstick is a new addition; she wasn't wearing that when I was inspecting her teeth. She has on a high-necked white blouse, a long ruffled purple skirt, and a black fur coat that doesn't seem fake. On anyone else, clothes like that would look hideously old-fashioned, but she's tall enough and gorgeous enough to pull it off. Anyway, I like that she has her own look: Victorian goth.

Her eyes lock on mine; she smiles, and a shiver runs lightly down my spine as she walks over. That same floaty feeling I had at the end of her appointment washes through me. Like I'm not in control of my thoughts. Like I'm going to do or say something ridiculously inappropriate in her presence.

Get a grip, Damian, I tell myself sternly, clutching my Scotch glass so tightly it's liable to shatter. *It's just one date, and nothing's going to happen. Especially not what your dick is hoping for.*

'Hey, Dr Rhodes.' Florence grins at me, shrugs off her coat, and swings into the banquette beside me. 'Sorry I'm late, bus issues.' She pulls her long black hair forward over one shoulder, and I breathe in the scent of dried roses. It smells like nostalgia.

Reluctantly, I drag my eyes from her to glance at my

watch. It's 7.06 p.m.

'You're not late,' I say. 'I was way too early.'

She crosses her legs and smiles properly at me. God, I'm a sucker for good teeth and hers are almost perfect, apart from a slightly twisted left lateral incisor.

'I'm usually early too,' she says. 'You know what they say, the early bird catches the wriggly worm.' She arches a dark eyebrow suggestively, and I almost choke on the mouthful of Scotch I've just taken.

I swallow painfully as my brain processes the fact that she's openly flirting with me. And that I don't have any condoms ... Wait, why am I even thinking like that? Even if I am attracted to her, we would need to go out on a few dates at least before anything physical happened. I'm not the kind of guy that has one-night stands. I prefer to wait and see if there's relationship potential there first. It's kind of a rigid rule for me. So I'm not going to have sex with someone I just met.

'What do you want to drink?' I rasp, trying not to let any of my inner turmoil show as I slide the menu over to Florence.

'Hmm, let's see.' She peruses the menu thoughtfully, tapping her plump lower lip with a long purple fingernail.

I stare unabashedly, my cock twitching in my jeans. *So much for not thinking about sex.*

'I think I'll have a Bloody Mary.' She winks at me conspiratorially, but I don't get the joke.

'Right. Back in a tick.'

I saunter up to the bar to order, feeling more confident now that she's here. It could also be the two drams of whisky—I'm slightly fried.

'Can I get a Bloody Mary and a large glass of water? Thanks.'

The barman smirks. 'Pacing yourself, mate?'

I don't think he should be commenting on my drinking habits, but he's right. What if I need to perform? *Stop it, Damian. You are not having sex tonight.*

'Something like that,' I reply with a thin smile.

Florence is busily messaging someone on her phone and smiling to herself when I head back to the table, carrying the drinks, and my chest tightens in alarm. *I knew it, she's way too pretty not to have other options. Or maybe she's got a boyfriend and is considering this a 'just friends' type of date?*

'Here you go.' I place the red aromatic cocktail in front of her, trying not to show I'm bothered.

'Thanks.'

We clink glasses and say 'slainte'. She eyes my drink of choice curiously but doesn't comment.

I take several gulps of water to clear my head, which is suddenly fuzzy as fuck, while she takes a small sip of her

Bloody Mary and places it back on the table.

I know I shouldn't ask who she was messaging, but the question is burning a hole in my brain. *Do you have a boyfriend? Do you have a boyfriend?*

'Do you know the history of the Bloody Mary?' Florence says conversationally. 'It's quite interesting.'

I shake my head. 'Nope.'

'Well, Bloody Mary was the nickname given to Mary Tudor in the sixteenth century because when she became queen, she burned over 300 Protestants at the stake.' Florence twirls the swizzle stick around in her drink.

'So it was named after her?'

'No, it originated in Paris in 1921, thanks to a bartender, Fernand Petiot—or Pete, as he told me to call him. He had Americans visiting his bar with their canned tomato juice and Russians fleeing the revolution, bringing in vodka. One night, someone wanted a hangover cure. So he mixed them together, added some spice, and voilà! It was a match made in heaven.'

She smiles at me and takes the tiniest sip of her drink. The ruby liquid merely moistens her lips. For all her talk about Bloody Marys, she doesn't seem that keen about drinking her own.

'You seem clued-up. Do you have a history degree or something?' I ask.

She hitches a shoulder and smiles. 'I'm just interested in learning about the past, and I read a lot of historical novels. What about you? Do you read?'

'Ah, yeah, I'm mainly into horror and Gothic fiction.'

Florence perks up. 'Oooh yes, me too. The darker and spookier, the better.'

A somewhat competitive discussion ensues on different titles, but I have to concede defeat. She's read far more than I have, and I'm impressed by the way she can condense a plot into two or three sentences, essentially plucking out the heart of the story and making me intrigued to read it. I make a note on my phone of several books to download later on. Our conversation flows easily. As well as being attractive, Florence is intelligent, witty, and confidently flirtatious. It's early days, but she's ticking all the right boxes for me, which is surprising.

It's only when I've excused myself to use the men's and running through what we've said (being a dentist, I have a good memory for small talk) that I realise she's said something a bit off. Florence made it sound like she knew the guy who invented the Bloody Mary—'Pete, as he told me to call him,' she'd said. But she would have to be over 100 years old now if she knew him back then. I chuckle a little to myself as I finish and zip up my jeans. A slip of the tongue. She's so into her history that she's imagined herself there in Paris. That's kind of endearing.

Returning from the men's, I see Florence's glass is now empty, and she's twirling a lock of her black hair around her finger. I slide back into the booth, and she leans towards me, our shoulders nearly touching. 'You were thirsty after all,' I say teasingly.

'Always,' she replies with a low husky chuckle. A swoony feeling and a strong desire to kiss her slide through me. My inner debate fires up again.

I really like her. Should I suggest coming back to mine? But we've only just met, it's too soon.

My stomach muscles tense painfully with indecision, and it feels like I've eaten rocks.

Then I hear Florence's voice saying, 'Relax, Dr Rhodes.' I glance at her, and she says, 'There's no need to stress.'

But she must be speaking really softly as I can't see her lips moving. Still, it's nice that she's trying to put me at ease.

'OK,' I say, and she gives a small chuckle.

A warm glow—a bit like the whisky, but without the burning—spreads over my torso, and there's a soft persistent pressure on my upper back, like fingers massaging my shoulder blades. But when I look down, her hands are in her lap. Weird. I close my eyes, not analysing for once and enjoying this sudden relaxed state. I usually operate on a medium to high level of anxiety, partly because of how I'm wired and partly due to a traumatic experience from a few years ago. Even after visiting my therapist, I can't remember feeling so loose, so devil-may-care. Those two glasses of Scotch must really be kicking in.

Florence slips her hand onto my thigh underneath the table and lets it rest there lightly. I like that a lot. It suggests she's interested too, and I'm all for women making the first move. Her mauve lips touch the edge of my ear, and I shiver involuntarily.

'Sooooo do you want another water?' she whispers. 'Or do you want to come back to mine?'

Her hand moves higher towards my groin. 'Definitely yours,' I whisper back, not bothering to disguise my eagerness.

'Excellent,' she says, lightly nuzzling my earlobe. I stifle a moan as my cock stiffens. Florence giggles softly as if she knows exactly what's happening in my jeans right now.

Hardly knowing what's going on, except that I have a desperate need to be alone with her (and preferably without clothes), I rise and she hands me my coat, which I fold and place strategically over my crotch.

The barman gives me a wink and a thumbs up as we head downstairs, out of the bar, and into the cold night air, which slaps my cheeks hard; I start to think practically. *This is really happening, Damian. You're going to hers. You need a condom. Why the* fuck *didn't you bring a condom?*

At this point, I don't really care where she lives. She could stay in Fife, for all I care, as long as there's a Sainsbury's in the vicinity.

Florence loops her arm through mine as we head to the bus stop. 'By the way', she says, 'in case you're wondering, I live in the Old Town. There's a Sainsbury's down the road, and I don't have a boyfriend.'

CHAPTER 4

Damian insists on popping to the supermarket beforehand, so I give him our Ramsay Garden address and instructions to knock on the black downstairs door when he arrives—*not* the red one at the top of the stairs.

I almost told him that he didn't need to buy condoms, that I can't get pregnant, but I'm not supposed to know that he's buying them.

It was kind of cool, but a little disconcerting, to discover that I could hear his thoughts and project mine to him too at The Brief Encounter. Apparently, vampire mental powers improve with age, but I've never been able to use telepathy until tonight. And it's odd that it occurred at the bar and not at my dentist appointment. Damian did have a couple of glasses of whisky, though. Perhaps it loosened his brain cells?

Anyway, it suits my purposes to have him turn up later as I need to check Sadie's not lurking around like the fun police. She'll get all unholier-than-thou and remind me that I'm supposed to be keeping a low profile. But I've been doing that for decades, and I'm sick of it. Why shouldn't I enjoy myself a little? Besides, Sadie is a hypocrite—she gets lots of action on a regular basis from her thrall. It's safe to say that after a century, our friendship is well out of its honeymoon phase.

Inserting my key in the lock, I gently ease open the front door. In the hallway, I shrug off my fur coat. I didn't need to wear it for warmth, but Damian would have been overly curious as to why I was wearing a thin blouse in November.

Removing my boots, I zoom off to the lounge in my stockings. I tend to fly around the flat when I'm in a hurry as it's faster than walking. And I want to create a candlelit ambiance in my lair for my rendezvous with Damian. The lounge is almost in total darkness, apart from the soft glow of city lights through the double bay windows. But with my night vision, I can see at a glance that it's empty without needing to switch on the main light. Good, no Sadie on patrol; she must be in her room.

I'm about to glide back into the hallway when the black leather chair in the corner swings around slowly in a rather dramatic fashion, and I'm caught midhover. 'Hello, witch,' drawls Sadie in her smoky voice.

Shit, caught. I lower gently to the carpet and stand there guiltily, like a schoolgirl called to the headmistress's office.

Sadie crosses her Adidas-tracksuited legs and taps out a red-varnished staccato on the arm of the chair. Her matching red crop top rides up slightly to reveal a pierced belly button.

'And where have you been, Miss Hughes?'

'I had an appointment,' I say sulkily. I turn to walk away but am gently pulled into the room, my body submitting to her will. *Dammit, I hate it when she does that.*

Sadie leans forward, the ends of her blonde bob swinging, and picks up a glass tumbler filled with liquid from the coffee table. She takes a sip and licks her lips. It swirls like alcohol. But from the luminescence and the scent, I know it isn't.

'This late? An appointment with whom?'

'No business of yours.'

Unlike Hester, who respects my privacy, Sadie gleefully sifts through my memories and I have no choice in the matter. Even more annoying is the fact that I can't block her. Her mental abilities are too strong.

'Pretty little liar,' she purrs. 'You were on a date.' She takes another sip, swishes it around her mouth, and swallows, watching my reaction.

That had better not be the last of the blood. I was going to drink that before Damian arrived. *But I'm not going to ask for some ... I'm. Not. Going. To. Ask.*

'Where's Hester?' I say weakly, changing the subject before I cave like she wants me to.

'At her method acting class.' Sadie and I exchange a smirk. No matter how much animosity there is between us lately, we do agree on one thing: Hester's acting hobby is hilarious. She's obsessed with the theatre, but afraid of being in the spotlight. If there's even a whiff of her having to read aloud or perform a scene with another actor, she diverts the teacher's attention to someone else. She seems more interested in listening and taking notes.

Apparently feeling friendlier towards me, Sadie extends the tumbler, and I'm allowed to clutch it and take a desperate gulp. The lukewarm blood caresses my throat, and I let out a sigh. 'Thanks, I needed that.'

'So this Damian Rhodes is your dentist?' Sadie takes the glass from my hand and leans back in the chair, her eyes boring into mine, looking amused.

I shrug nonchalantly. 'Yes, so what? He's hot.'

Sadie narrows her eyes. 'You're not seriously thinking of seeing him again?'

'Uh ...' I stare up at the ceiling, desperate for her not to find out he's actually on his way to the flat. Luckily, she's more interested in telling me off.

'Floss, you know you can't get involved with a human—'

'What about you and Elliott?' I interrupt with a scoff.

Sadie met her thrall in 1983. He was head over heels the moment she sank her fangs into him—Sadie's feelings, however, remain a well-guarded mystery, possibly even to her.

She frowns. 'Elliott doesn't count,' she says quickly. 'Fine, have your little fun tonight. But you'll have to get me or Hester to memory-wipe him afterwards.'

I don't reply.

'You have to, Floss. For his own safety.'

I grind my teeth together and can't resist thinking, *So explain to me again why you're allowed to be with Elliott.*

She rolls her eyes and projects her stock answer into my mind: *It's a business relationship, you know that. Elliott supplies us with blood from student donors. Without him, we'd have to resort to feeding on humans, and none of us want to do that anymore.*

I personally think we've become too reliant on Elliott as our blood supplier. But as much as I hate to admit it, Sadie is right. My life is too complicated to get involved with a human. I should have left Damian alone and not encouraged him to ask me out. And I definitely shouldn't have invited fresh blood around to our flat; it's risky for him.

But he's got me aroused and itching to play with him a little, and he'll be safe with me. I'm not going to hurt him. It's also fun that I can read his mind, and I want to do it again. And who knows, he might be up for some bite action. After all, he yanked a tooth out of that guy the other day without anaesthetic and hardly batted an eyelid ...

'Anyway, enough about hot human dentists. There's something more important to discuss,' Sadie continues out loud as though my love life is now satisfactorily resolved. 'We need to have a flat meeting.'

'Why?'

She takes a sip of blood, and her eyes rest steadily on mine. 'Because I had a disturbing report from Elliott today. One of his regular male donors was bitten last night in Bonnington after leaving a party. So it seems a certain Victorian gentleman may be visiting the city.'

A finger of fear worms its way into my ribcage and curls around my cold, dead heart. Bonnington is on the other side of town but not that far away.

'W-was he drained?'

'No, but the gentleman took a big, long drink. Luckily, someone found the student lying in an alleyway and called an ambulance. He was given a blood transfusion at the hospital. Elliott visited this morning and the student told him what happened. The description he gave matches.'

'Fuck.'

'Yeah, it's a bit too close for comfort. So we need to discuss it with Hester, to make sure she shields you. I don't want to take any chances.'

'It may not be *him* ...' I can't say his name. It's like Shakespeare's *Macbeth*; if I say it, something bad will happen.

'No, it may not be. But if it is ...'

'Don't say it,' I warn her. '*Don't* say his name.'

'*Alexander*,' she intones, and I groan. Shit, she said it. Now we're all doomed!

A knock sounds from downstairs, and Sadie angles her head sharply towards the noise. *Who's that?*

I start backing away from her one step at a time while she's distracted.

Ah, gotta go. My dentist has arrived. Thanks for the drink.

Sadie scowls. But before she has a chance to remind me again of my vampiric responsibilities, I'm flying down the staircase that leads to my lair. As soon as I'm out of her presence, my mood picks up, and anticipation skitters down my spine. Carpe diem. If my vengeful sire is close to discovering my whereabouts, I may as well have some fun before he does.

CHAPTER 5

Florence | London, 1888

'It has been said that the East End is a "terra incognita for respectable citizens". But I think parts of it are rather underrated,' remarks Dr Dryden. 'And especially pleasant for strolling around on summer evenings.'

My interview has reared off on a tangent. I have no idea what 'terra' whatsit is, but I don't need a gent telling me that the East End isn't all that bad. It's autumn now, so the worst of the London heat is over. But Spitalfields still stinks—morning and night, in any season.

'Since you like the East End so much, maybe you should try living there and not in Belgravia, sir,' I can't help saying stiffly, which earns me a low chuckle in reply.

I'm surprised that, yet again, he's amused at me speaking my mind and that he has a sense of humour—even though it's so dry you could use it for kindling to light a fire. Remarkably, for my latest snide comment, he doesn't throw me out for impertinence but suggests showing me around the house instead. *So does that mean I've got the job? I have no clue.*

'My aunt said the position is live-in. Is that the case?' I enquire as we start down the hallway.

'Yes, that's correct,' he clarifies, throwing open a door on the right. 'This is the parlour.'

I peer inside. It too is a dim room like the rest of the house, thanks to heavy black velvet drapes being partially drawn. The only interesting furniture is an overstuffed emerald-green sofa that looks comfortable to sit on.

He pulls the door shut, and we continue down the dark nondescript hallway without any family photos until we reach the end, which has a door. He gestures for me to open it. 'The kitchen is through here.'

'Oh,' I say, wondering why he's showing me the kitchen. Would I have to clean it?

The kitchen, I'm relieved to discover, is pristine and has a gleaming row of copper pans. But it doesn't look like it's ever been used. The range is stone cold.

'I don't have a cook at present,' says Dr Dryden from behind my left shoulder. 'It's difficult to get good help these days.'

He's standing so close to me the air between us seems to tighten, and my skin hums with awareness. I step away, pretending to study some teacups with a tiny pink-and-gold rose pattern, though I can still feel him, like a shadow at my back.

'What do you do for meals then?' I ask, turning to look at him.

The corner of his mouth quirks. 'My son and I tend to dine out.'

I glance up at the ceiling. *His very quiet son.*

'I'm used to cooking for myself. A bit of cheese on toast suits me,' I tell him, hoping to sway his mind and give me the position.

'An independent spirit, I see. Good, good. That's what I'm looking for in a governess.' From that, it seems I'm still in the running. But there's something about the way Dr Dryden's looking at me that is shiver inducing, and the fine hairs on my arms rise. I would go so far to describe it as a *'hungry look'*, but I did just mention cheese on toast, and it's nearly time for lunch.

'After you, Miss Hughes.' Dr Dryden stands aside to let me pass, and as I do, he rocks forward and sniffs me. Only slightly, but it's definitely sniffing. Shame courses through me. Do I smell bad? I had a good wash before I came here.

He doesn't offer to show me upstairs and walks towards the front door. It seems the tour—and the interview—is over.

The thought of going back to Aunt Ivy, to our rickety flat with its peeling wallpaper and communal outhouse, makes me panic when we're standing by the door.

'Please, sir, I know it's bold of me to ask. But can you tell me if I've got the position or not? If I haven't, I'd rather know. I hate being kept in suspense.'

'Do you now?' Dr Dryden looks down at me thoughtfully. 'Hold out your arm then.'

'Excuse me?'

'Your arm please, Miss Hughes.'

Hesitantly, I extend my right arm, and he pushes the sleeve of my dress up carefully and trails a cool finger down my warm skin. His icy touch is thrilling, and I can't help shuddering a little.

Dr Dryden studies the inside of my lily-white wrist. He prods a forefinger at the network of pale-blue veins.

'Does your skin bruise easily?'

The question confuses me, but I sense the answer I give will help him decide whether to offer me the position. But why does he want to know? Is it something to do with his son?

'I-I'm not sure, sir. I don't think so. No more than anyone else's.'

'Are you healthy?'

'Yes, sir.'

'Do you have any conditions?'

'No, sir.'

I realise then that this is a health examination, not some excuse to touch me, and my cheeks flush a little for reading more into it than I should.

'Very well.' He drops my arm, and I pull down my sleeve. 'I've decided that you will do very nicely. I mean ...' He clears his throat softly. 'That you would be a welcome addition to the Dryden household.'

My heart lifts, and I can't help the grin that spreads over my face. 'Really, sir?'

He nods. 'Really, Miss Hughes.'

Wait till Aunt Ivy hears this. I'm going up in the world!

'If you'd like to tell me your *real* address, I'll write to your aunt and confirm it. I'll also let you know what date you'll be starting.'

'Of course, sir.' I tell him the address, and then I'm being shown outside onto the stoop. He says a quick goodbye and is about to close the door.

'Sir?'

He opens the door a crack, and an eye glints at me. The rest of him blends in with the darkness beyond the door. 'Yes?'

'Can I just ask, why? The reason why you chose me, I mean.'

There's a long pause. 'I find you ... refreshing. Good day, Miss Hughes. I will be in touch.'

The door closes abruptly, and I stand there for a moment, lost for words.

Refreshing? I've never been called that by a man before. 'Bookish', 'mouthy', and once I was called a 'prig', but never 'refreshing'. Aunt Ivy is going to chuckle when I tell her that.

It's only when I'm on the omnibus heading back to Spitalfields that I realise he hasn't told me anything about his son whatsoever.

***

Aunt Ivy, as expected, is thrilled that I was chosen for the position and is patting herself on the back for giving me a leg up in society, even if it is by underhanded means. It relieves her of some of the responsibility of feeding and clothing me. God knows she's finding it hard enough to feed and clothe herself.

'Dr Dryden found out I live in Spitalfields, and he still chose me. What do you think that means?' I ask her that evening when we're sat in front of the fire, toasting bread. Now that the excitement has worn off, the slight misgiving that I had at the interview about working for him has turned into full-blown foreboding.

Aunt Ivy swivels her fork slowly, toasting her bread

evenly in the low flame, firelight shadows dancing on the faded green living room walls.

'He's not a snob. That's all it means.'

'But he didn't even tell me about his son or show me upstairs.' *He sniffed me* … 'I have a bad feeling about him. I don't think I should work there.'

Aunt Ivy gives me an incredulous look. 'Turn down an offer of a live-in position and a good salary? He's a doctor. A respectable man.'

I stare silently at my toasted bread, which is starting to blacken around the edges. Am I being silly? I can't help how I feel. My gut is telling me that there's something not right.

'He chose you because you're special,' Aunt Ivy continues, transferring the steaming toast to her plate with nimble fingers. 'Like I chose you from your ten brothers and sisters in Whitechapel. If I hadn't, where do you think you'd be now?'

I shrug.

'Dead or selling your body on the streets, no doubt. My sister married for love, and she's suffering for it. Last I heard, she'd taken up with the gin—and that never ends well.' She scrapes butter onto her toast angrily to make her point. 'So I won't hear another word. You're going to him, Florence, and that's final. It will be the making of you, mark my words.'

My bread is now more char than toast, but I hardly notice. A knot of fear lodges in my stomach.

But what other choice do I have other than to marry well? However, even that is proving impossible. I have looks enough, but I lack money and connections, and prosperous men don't marry for beauty alone. No, Aunt Ivy is right: beggars can't be choosers, and I'd be a fool to look a gift horse in the mouth.

CHAPTER 6

Damian | Edinburgh, present day

Florence's bedroom could be a museum display—apart from the fact there's no explanatory sign telling you about the occupant's life or the date they lived there. *She wasn't joking when she said she was interested in the past ...*

I've read about people who feel like they belong in another era, but I've never met anyone who believes it to such an extent. Until now.

To the left is a fireplace with a black lead grate filled with glowing white candles, and in front of it sit two squat leather armchairs. To the right stands a bookcase stocked with leather-bound books. A plush crimson-and-gold oriental rug covers the dark polished floorboards, and atop it, next to the bookcase, rests a four-poster bed with thick, carved wooden posts. A freestanding armoire with a changing screen stands on the far left-hand side. The entire room is painted deep red, even the ceiling.

The flickering candles, the tick of the antique clock on the mantel, and the shifting shadows in the corners are giving me serious Edgar Allan Poe vibes.

'This is ... dedicated,' I say, looking around. *And slightly spooky. Who lives like this in the twenty-first century?*

'Do you like it?' Florence is standing right in front of me, and I blink. Wasn't she over by the fireplace a second ago? She's watching me carefully, as if to gauge my reaction.

'I do. But I feel underdressed, like I should be wearing an evening suit or something,' I joke.

Florence looks at me steadily and says deadpan, 'Or you could wear your birthday suit.'

There's no mistaking *that* as a come-on, and my cock thickens in my jeans. But I simply smirk at her, and she gives me a coy smile.

Yes, I'm playing the age-old 'hard to get' game, which is my fail-safe method when it comes to women (but I also want to keep my clothes on for as long as possible, as it's freaking cold in here). However, I have a box of condoms in my coat pocket, and cold or not, I'm itching to kiss her glossy lips and roll around naked in that cool four-poster. And chat some more about books afterwards, of course ...

'Would you like something to drink? I have some port.' Florence swishes over to the sideboard and uncaps a crystal decanter, and I catch a whiff of plums and spice. The scent of dried roses is also more potent in here, and it's making me think of graveyards and church altars. She must have a dish of potpourri stashed somewhere.

'I'm fine, thanks,' I say, looking for somewhere to put my coat.

Suddenly, it's removed from my arms, and a hand snakes around my waist. I glance down to see purple fingernails stroking my rock-hard length. How on earth Florence managed to get behind me so quickly, I don't know. But her hand on my dick feels amazing. OK, she's a bit quirky, and she lives in a museum. But if she wants to move things along, that's fine with me.

Her other hand tugs gently at my hair, and my head lolls back as if my spine were Plasticine. I feel like I'm drunk, though I'm sure I declined the port. Or did I? Did we sit in the armchairs by the fireside candles and talk? My head is all fuzzy, and I can't remember. Florence is kissing and licking at my neck as she strokes me, and I groan at how good it all feels.

'Shall we lie down, Dr Rhodes?' she asks, massaging my straining cock.

The friction is too pleasurable, and my balls start tightening. *Do not come in your jeans, Damian. Premature ejaculation is not appreciated on a first date.*

I glance at the four-poster with its red satin cover and array of plump white pillows and nod quickly, hoping I can hold out until we're in bed.

To my relief, she removes her magical fingers, and I gain a semblance of control.

'Unless you prefer ...'

I look down again to see Florence, now on her knees, undoing my belt buckle. My eyes widen. But she gives me a sexy grin and starts unzipping my jeans, her mouth inches from my erection, which is throbbing and twitching like it's got a mind of its own.

Before I know it, my jeans are sliding down my thighs, and I'm in my grey boxer briefs. I panic slightly, feeling like I'm losing control of this situation. *Was I ever in control of it?*

But she smiles up at me. 'Relax, Dr Rhodes.'

'I thought we were lying down?'

'I changed my mind,' she purrs, kissing my thigh. 'Mmm, you're very biteable.'

Florence nips at my flesh with her teeth, which tickles, but I don't mind. She can do what she likes down there and seems to be doing just that as she licks up and down my inner thigh and gently squeezes my balls through my briefs.

God, that feels nice. I exhale, my anxiety easing off.

'Cool,' I hear her say. 'I'll keep going then.'

Momentarily confused about where her voice is coming from, I blink as my briefs are eased down over my swollen length. My cock quivers at being exposed to the cold air.

I tense, waiting for her tongue to warm it up. But she doesn't. There's a short pause in proceedings below, and insecurity shoots through me. *Is it too small? Was her last boyfriend's cock bigger? Does it look weird?*

Then my boxer briefs are travelling down my thighs to join my jeans on the floor, and she starts kissing my thigh again and cupping my naked balls. I exhale in relief, feeling like I've passed some kind of test.

Risking a glance, I watch as Florence's kisses move closer and closer to the tip of my wet cock, and my entire body trembles with anticipation. I run my tongue over my dry lips. So much for my rigid rule—here I am with my dick out and my good intentions around my ankles. But I'm in too deep to back out now. Besides, I'm beyond the point of caring. I *want* her to suck me off. It's going to feel so incredibly—I jerk as a sharp, stinging pain shoots through my upper thigh.

'Ow! What the fuck!'

'Sorry,' Florence murmurs, clutching my bare buttocks in both hands. She presses her lips tightly against the spot on my thigh.

Did she scratch me with one of her nails?

But it felt more like *needles* ... A wave of dizziness washes over me as I feel blood being suctioned from the wound, and Florence makes a gulping noise. Oh god, I knew it was too good to be true; of course there's something weird about her.

'Stop it!' I push Florence's head away from my thigh and hurriedly pull up my boxer briefs and jeans, my cock shrivelling like a day-old sausage.

She wipes her mouth and stands to face me.

I grab my coat off the bed. 'I'm going.'

Florence swallows; the pupils of her eyes are so dilated that they appear black with a tiny rim of violet.

'Please don't leave. I'm really sorry about that,' she says softly, taking a step towards me.

I take a step back. 'It's not you. It's me. I'm just not into kink ...' *Especially bloodplay!*

'Please stay, Damian. We can talk ...'

She smiles encouragingly, and I stare at her teeth—her canines are extra long and sharply pointed. Before I've had a chance to get a good look at them, she shuts her mouth hurriedly.

I'm so sorry. I didn't mean to scare you.

Florence's voice whispers in my mind, but her lips are still pressed together.

Things suddenly click into place: her clothes, this room, the slip-up about the Bloody Mary in 1921, the biting, bloodsucking and telepathy.

Fuck, she's a vampire. But vampires don't exist! Are you going to stick around and debate that with her, numbnuts?

Heart pounding, I make a lunge for the door and stumble out into the short hallway. Reaching the front entrance, I check behind me. The vampire isn't following, thank God. Bursting out the door into the crisp night air, I sprint down The Mound like the hounds of hell are after me. A strange energy flows through my limbs, and I run full pelt with my lungs on fire, covering the mile and a half to my apartment on Leith Walk in ten minutes flat.

With trembling fingers, I double-lock the door and pull across the safety chain, then collapse on my living room couch, gasping for breath.

What. The. Actual. Fuck?

CHAPTER 7

Biting Damian was wrong. I knew it was, but I couldn't help myself. Once the taste of his blood hit my tongue and slipped down my throat, I wanted more and more. It was just a moment, but it was enough. He caught a glimpse of my fangs too. Now he's bolted out the door before I could stop him. *Fuck.*

There's only one thing I can do to make this situation right: wipe his memory. But there's one problem with that: I've never done it before.

Panicking, I run for my big book of practical lessons for vampires, heave it out of the bookshelf, and blow the dust off it. The Gothic font is hard to read, so I've never really bothered with it much, but I flip to the section I want: Memory Erasure. The first sentence has a foreboding warning: *If performed incorrectly, this procedure will result total amnesia. Proceed with caution!*

It's a risk, but I have to try. I can't let him know about me. I struggle to make out the brief list of instructions, but it seems straightforward. Luckily, Damian's blood is still in my system. So all I have to do is isolate the memory I want to erase, recite the Lament of Unknowing, and extinguish the candles one by one.

I quickly complete the ritual and sit by the fireplace with bergamot-scented smoke drifting around me, feeling a bit bereft. Now Damian will wake up with a hangover, thinking he had too much to drink after a night out with his mates. He'll remember my dental appointment, but nothing about asking me out, going on a date with me at the bar, or coming back to my lair—not to mention the biting, bloodsucking, and fangs. He may feel mildly anxious but will put it down to a stressful week at work. *It was the right thing to do.*

But now I have to face a long, lonely night without a yummy dentist to snuggle up with. And I need to calm down after this harrowing experience. Removing my blouse and skirt, I haul out the Dyson from the armoire and begin hoovering the rug in my corset and stockings. Sadie prefers dancing, and Hester running, but cleaning is my go-to for expending nervous energy. I have a large bag full of eco-friendly sprays and microfibre cloths kept expressly for this purpose.

Hoovering done, I start methodically dusting the mantelpiece.

Wipe.

Wipe.

Wipe.

Speaking of my flatmates, they would be highly amused if they found out I accidentally drank Damian's blood and he ran away. Sadie especially—I'd get the 'I told you so' speech from her, which I really don't want to hear. So I'm not going to say anything.

But meeting Damian was a bright spot in the decades of darkness, and now even that has been taken away from me. I know already, from the heaviness in my chest, that I'm going to be depressed about this for at least a year until I can see him at my next dental appointment.

Wipe.

Wipe.

Wipe.

Why can't I have a normal loving relationship with someone I'm attracted to? I bemoan for what feels like the hundredth time this decade. *Because you're a vampire, you ninny. The sooner you get that through your thick skull, the better ...*

After I've finished cleaning, I unhook my corset, roll down my stockings, and put on a fresh cotton nightgown. Once I'm settled in bed, I bring up the first book of a new spicy paranormal romance series on my Kindle that I've been looking forward to sinking my teeth into. This should make me feel a bit better. Reading about vampires freely feeding on humans is my guilty pleasure.

Except I can't forget about Damian.

My mind wanders as certain juicy scenes replay in my head: the way he moaned when I stroked him and how his heart pumped fiercely—all that lovely blood rushing through his veins. He was putty in my hands.

And his lovely thick cock, oh my god. My pussy starts throbbing just thinking about it.

He was so adorable, worrying that it was too small or weird-looking. I wanted to reassure him that as cocks went, his was five stars, but that would have meant explaining how I could read his thoughts.

Anyway, then I bit him, and he tore off like a frightened rabbit. Remembering that part isn't good for my mental health. I swipe to the next page and try to focus.

But Damian's fear was palpable, and the memory of his shocked face is gnawing at me. It hurts that he reacted that way, but I don't blame him in the slightest. Being confronted with a vampire is challenging at the best of times, and I'm sure when one is latched onto your thigh with your tackle out, it's downright terrifying. Oh well, he won't remember anything about our date when he wakes up, so there's no point wallowing.

***

At 3 a.m., I throw down the Kindle, having devoured the book and been left wanting. There was too much witty banter and not enough bloodsucking for my liking. But the sex scenes were arousing, and it has my mind wandering to Damian again. If I hadn't bitten him, we might have given each other a satisfying orgasm (even if the condoms didn't get used, *some* kind of action would have been nice), then had a lovely cuddle before he fell asleep in my arms, and I watched over him through the night. The longing for that overwhelms me in its intensity.

To the point that I start fantasising. What if I start over, make another appointment, and encourage Damian to ask me out again? But then instead of biting him, I bring him round veeery slowly to the idea of me being a vampire. He's into Gothic fiction and horror, so he might be OK with it?

But if Sadie is right and Alexander is in Edinburgh, it's more dangerous to get involved with a human. He's vindictive and liable to hurt anything I care about. It's a risk, but I can check if Alexander's still in the city easily enough, and Hester can shield me if he is until he goes away again.

Besides, it's the middle of the night and the perfect time to do a little bloodseeking.

The castle has tight security after hours, so I don't go up there. Scott Monument is a better alternative—it's the tallest structure near our flat and my usual vantage point if we get word of Alexander lurking around. The height gives me better range. On the occasions I picked up on him, Hester shielded me until the coast was clear. But it's disturbing that he won't stop hunting me—he's like a dog with a bone.

From one of the drawers of the armoire I pull out a pair of black leggings, a long-sleeved black top, and a balaclava. After donning these, I pull on my boots.

Checking the street is empty, I slip out the back gate, shoot down Mound Place, and fly across the train tracks, moving too fast to be seen by the human eye. Technically, I could fly up Scott Monument, but I like climbing because it's meditative.

Having scaled the sixty-metre structure, I walk around on the topmost balcony beneath the Gothic spire. Finding the most sheltered spot, I remove my balaclava and stand there with my eyes closed, focusing, the cold breeze lifting my hair. Bloodseeking is akin to kind of *pushing* my senses out into the city, then farther into the suburbs and surrounding countryside, seeking to feel the tug of my blood bond with Alexander.

Absolutely nothing.

Unless he's hiding out in Queensferry? I push west, to the

edge of my limits, and there's no sense of him there either.

I'm completely reassured by my bloodseeking sweep—he's not here.

***

'I couldn't detect him anywhere in Edinburgh or in the near vicinity. If he was here, he isn't now,' I inform Sadie that night during our flat meeting. Hester and I are perched on the leather couch as Sadie presides over us in her revolving chair. We all have 'Bloody' Marys placed on the coffee table between us. As Hester says, 'We need sustenance. Otherwise, we'll get hangry.' Sadie's flat meetings are notorious for running overtime *and* having multiple items on the agenda. Luckily for Hester and I, I've pre-empted Sadie's request for me to bloodseek, so I can report confidently on the first item.

'Good. Thank you, Floss,' she says, making a note on her iPad. 'But I'd like you on bloodseeking duty all next week please. Just to make sure. And Hester you can shield her.'

I resist a frustrated eye roll. She's being super vigilant, but I suppose it's in her best interests to do so. Sadie and Hester are accomplices, so all three of us are at risk.

'Fine, if you think it's necessary. But I'm pretty sure he's fucked off back to London, where he belongs,' I mutter.

'Noted. Thank you for being so accommodating, Floss,' Sadie says sarcastically. 'On to the next item.' She taps her iPad screen with a French-manicured index finger. As well as her newly polished nails, I note that she's rather overdressed for a flat meeting: lime-green crop top, black barely-there leather skirt, sheer tights, and black stilettos.

'Our blood is running low, so Elliott's coming over soon with a fresh supply. That should last us for two to three weeks as long as we don't guzzle it,' she states.

Ah, right, so her hot thrall's the reason she's all dressed up ...

Hester hears my thought and sniggers while Sadie shoots me a glare, having heard it too. She's highly sensitive about her relationship with Elliott and hates us making snide comments.

Sadie drains her glass, avoiding our eyes. 'That's it for tonight's meeting, so you can both go. Unless you want to tell us how your *acting lesson* went last night, Hester?' she says sharply.

Hester shakes her head, her long auburn plait brushing my arm. She's also highly sensitive about her hobby, so she won't be telling Sadie a thing. But she might tell me later, if I ask nicely.

I clear my throat. 'I'd like to raise another item.'

I decided when I was descending Scott Monument that I

should probably tell them my plans for Damian part 2 because they'll find out anyway. But I'll make it sound like it's a second date and not mention the bloodsucking on date 1.

Sadie glances at the time on her phone and frowns. 'Yes. What is it, Floss?'

Wow, OK. Elliott must be due any minute.

'Ah, yeah, so about that dentist—'

The doorbell chimes, and Sadie's face brightens momentarily before falling back into its usual droll expression.

'It's nothing important. It can wait, I suppose ...' I start, but Sadie is already up and out of her chair to answer the door.

'Send me a message, and I'll add it to the next agenda,' she throws over her shoulder.

'Keen much?' whispers Hester, and I giggle softly.

We listen as Elliott's sultry London accent floats in from the hallway. 'Fuck me, it's cold out there. 'Ello, gorgeous.'

There's the sound of a 'mwah' as lips smack against a cheek. 'Don't call me that and do not kiss me until I tell you that you can,' Sadie says gruffly in an admonishing tone.

A scuffling sound occurs, and then Sadie pokes her head into the lounge. 'We're going upstairs. He'll be back down shortly to say hello.'

When she's gone, I look at Hester and pull a face.

'He wants to become a vampire one day, and we need him,' she says matter-of-factly.

'Doesn't make it right.'

Elliott is bound to Sadie's will. She feeds from him and gives him enough of her venom to keep him hooked and ageless but won't turn him—even though he's been begging her to for nearly forty years.

'I know, it's fucked up, but Elliott is the only thing standing between us and feeding from humans. Do you want to start doing that again?' asks Hester.

Damian's fearful face flashes into my mind, and the Bloody Mary gurgles guiltily in my stomach.

'No, definitely not.'

CHAPTER 8

Florence | London, 1888

Dr Dryden's son is called Charlie, and he suffers from several debilitating conditions: an aversion to sunlight so he can't go outside, chronic anaemia, and insomnia. Since he has trouble sleeping at night, he naps for most of the day.

I learn this surprising, and somewhat distressing, information in Dr Dryden's study a week later when I start my governess position. 'So when am I to give him lessons if he's napping all day, sir?'

Dr Dryden leans back in his chair and steeples his fingers. He surveys me intensely over the tips. 'He's up around dusk. You'll need to work with him in the evening and nap during the day yourself.'

I'm confused by this reply. 'Like a night shift?'

'Exactly,' he clarifies. 'Think of everything as being in reverse. For instance, you'd read to him just before dawn.'

I blink at that. 'If you don't mind me saying so, sir, that sounds a little strange.'

Dr Dryden's thick eyebrows draw together. 'Strange, but something you think you can adapt to? Or too strange to even consider?'

I'm tempted to say the latter, but then I know that I'll be shown the door, and I'll have to explain to Aunty Ivy why I'm back. I can hear her voice now: *Just try it, Floss. Think of the child's needs ... and the money.*

'I suppose I could adapt,' I say slowly. 'I am a bit of a night owl, and your son can't help being ill. It must be difficult for him.'

Dr Dryden's demeanour visibly softens, and he smiles at me, but his eyes hold a tinge of sadness.

'It is difficult for him ... and for me. Thank you for being so accommodating, Florence. Would you like to meet Charlie now?'

I glance at the clock on the mantel, which is coming up on noon. 'Yes, but isn't he asleep?'

'I'll wake him briefly, and then you can settle in. I had some food delivered yesterday, so you can see to your lunch.'

'All right. Thank you, sir.' He doesn't seem to want me to prepare any lunch for him. And I am highly curious to meet his son. I think it's mostly Dr Dryden's impromptu health examination last time that has been worrying me. But now I understand why it was necessary: Charlie is sickly, and his father doesn't want me passing on an illness that he can't fight off.

As we're ascending the stairs, me clutching my battered suitcase of meagre belongings, I feel more confident about broaching the subject. 'Excuse me for asking, sir, but has Charlie been like this for a while?'

'Yes, his symptoms started a few years ago. His mother was similarly afflicted. Sleeping during the day is the only way that Charlie can function, which is why I encourage it. But his mother insisted on "living normally", so to speak. Her system gradually weakened until she ... succumbed.'

Two steps ahead of me, he grips the banister tightly for a moment, then continues on up the carpeted stairs.

'I'm so sorry for your loss, sir.' How awful. *Did something happen because she tried to go outside?* I wonder.

'Thank you, Florence. As it happens, I am working on a cure for Charlie.'

'I hope you will be successful, sir,' I say fervently.

We reach the top of the stairs, and he smiles down at me. I'm struck again by how handsome he is—and much too young to be a widower. 'I think I am close to finding one, Florence. Which is why I need your help.'

'Of course, sir. I'm glad to be of service.'

He nods. 'I've put you in the room next door to Charlie.

Sometimes he has bad dreams and needs comforting. I know it's out of the scope of a governess's duties, but as I conduct important experiments in my basement laboratory, I may be too busy to attend to him. I trust that you do not mind? You would only need to hold his hand and speak softly to him, and he will go back to sleep after a few moments.'

'I don't mind at all, sir.'

Poor little Charlie, he does sound in a bad way.

Now that I'm starting to get a feel for what's required of me, I'm eager for us to get along.

I set down my suitcase outside Charlie's room. Dr Dryden inches open the bedroom door and beckons me to follow him inside, then closes it behind us promptly. Charlie's room is considerably darker than the other rooms in the house due to the tightly drawn drapes. It's so dark in here that I'm struggling to make anything out. There's a light floral scent that's not unpleasant; it smells like rose water has been sprinkled around.

Taking a cautious step forward, I touch the edge of a rug with my foot and feel around in case there's something there that might trip me up. I consider asking Dr Dryden to light a candle, but as soon as I think that, his hand is placed on the small of my back. He has touched my wrist previously, so it's not too shocking. But still ... it gives me a funny tingle in my lower belly.

'Let me guide you,' he whispers. 'I would light a candle, but we will only be a minute.'

'All right,' I whisper back, thinking that he must have excellent eyesight as I can't see a blasted thing.

We inch forward slowly in the darkness, like participants in a blind dance ritual. The ridiculousness of the situation strikes me, and I smother a giggle before it can erupt. How awful if I laughed now! He would think me terribly rude and unfeeling when his son is so ill.

We come to a halt, and by then, my eyes have adjusted a little so I can make out the shape of a bed. I'm all at sea, but my searching fingers reach the comforting shore of a soft, plush bedcover. As soon as I'm anchored, Dr Dryden removes his hand from my back and whispers to someone at the top of the bed. There's a rustling as a figure shifts beneath the cover, and a thin quavering voice calls out, 'Is it evening, Papa?'

'Shh now, not for a few more hours. But your new governess is here. Miss Hughes. I wish for you to meet her.'

There's a silence for a few moments, as if Charlie is considering this.

'Very well, Papa,' he says wearily as if he would rather go back to sleep. 'Please sit down, Miss Hughes, so I can look at you.'

Surprised by this request, I hesitate. Surely, there needs to be a candle lit for that to happen?

But Dr Dryden presses lightly on my shoulder, and I sink dutifully onto the side of the bed, my heart thumping in my ribcage.

After a moment, there's more rustling. Then a pale face emerges out of the darkness, so close to mine that I can't help but shrink back in fear. But for some reason, I can't seem to move my limbs, they feel heavy as lead.

'Don't be alarmed, Miss Hughes. It's just me, Charlie.' The young boy's voice is as smooth as silk. A cool hand strokes lightly on top of mine, and a feeling of calm laps at the edges of my nervousness. I take a breath. 'Pleased to meet you.'

I strain to see him better, but Charlie's features are indistinguishable, except for a pair of glinting eyes that seem to be inspecting me.

'Yes, she will do, Papa,' he murmurs at last, and the pale face dissipates into the darkness, and there's further rustling as if he's lying back down. 'I will see you later this evening, Miss Hughes, for our lessons.' There's amusement in his tone.

'Y-yes, of course,' I stutter.

He yawns; then there's complete silence.

Dr Dryden has remained quietly by my side throughout this exchange and now puts a hand under my elbow, inviting me to stand.

'We'll go now,' he whispers in my ear.

Feeling as if I'm in a trance, I let him guide me across the room to the door. As soon as he opens it, I stumble through in a panic, feeling like I'm being watched. He closes the door promptly after us.

The dim landing seems almost brightly lit after the suffocating darkness, and I'm mightily relieved to be out of that nightmarish bedroom.

Without awaiting my opinion on what just transpired, Dr Dryden picks up my suitcase and gestures towards the door to the right of Charlie's. 'This is your room, Miss Hughes. You may spend the afternoon as you wish. But we will partake of supper together this evening. As I mentioned, my son and I usually dine out, but we will make an exception this once—to welcome you to our home.'

'So Charlie will be joining us?' I enquire, twisting the handle and lingering in the doorway.

'Oh, yes. He told me he is looking forward to it,' he replies, a small smile playing on his lips.

Did he? A shiver of unease rolls through me as I didn't hear Charlie say anything of the sort.

'Supper will be at six thirty sharp in the dining room.'

I nod, and Dr Dryden bids me good day, leaving me to my thoughts and mounting fears. Thankfully, the thick curtains are open in this room, and a shaft of sunlight reveals a pretty bedroom decorated with rose wallpaper and a large comfortable bed with a cream satin coverlet. But the lovely room does nothing to reassure me after the encounter I've just had with Charlie. I sit there on the bed, clutching my suitcase with trembling hands. What on earth has Aunt Ivy got me into?

CHAPTER 9

Damian | Edinburgh, present day

Exactly what took place after my date with Florence at The Brief Encounter is a blank. I can remember drinking whisky and chatting about books, then leaving the bar with her. The last memory I have is of us catching the bus together. I must have come home and passed out. Now I've woken up in the late afternoon with a thumping hangover. What a lightweight.

But when I retrieve my coat, which has been flung on the floor, I find a box of condoms and a Sainsbury's receipt in the pocket. The box is sealed, so it's unlikely that we had sex. Yet I can't remember buying them.

When I'm in the shower, I discover another inexplicable thing: a medium-sized purple bruise on my left upper thigh with two small blood-encrusted wounds in the centre of it. Flea bites? From someone's dog in the bar last night? I must've been scratching them in my sleep.

But as I soap the bruise, Florence's face springs to mind

for some reason, and I start feeling aroused. Sliding my slippery hand onto my stiff cock, I stroke lazily, picturing her parted glossy lips and her darting tongue circling my head. The image of her eagerly sucking while I grind my hips is so vivid that I come hard, shuddering against the shower wall.

After that, I decide I don't want to wait three days before messaging in my usual 'playing hard to get' fashion—not when I'm this attracted to her. But tonight is way too soon for another date. I need to let it breathe a little. What about tomorrow? Would she freak out if I invited her to my parents' place for Sunday lunch? We could come back to mine afterwards ...

I eagerly type a message as soon as I'm out of the shower. But it's much too long. I need to word it properly. By the time I send it after dinner, it's gone through several iterations. The final version being:

Hey Florence, I had a great time last night. Bit forward maybe, but any chance you're around tomorrow? I'm heading to my parents' for Sunday lunch at noon, but if you fancied joining, you'd be very welcome. Totally get it if that feels like too much. We could always hang out after instead? No pressure either way. Let me know :) D

Not expecting a reply straightaway, I throw my phone on the couch and run a hand shakily through my hair. My dick is tenting my joggers and throbbing like crazy again. What is it about this woman? She's driving me to distraction.

It's times like these that I wish I lived with a male flatmate. At least I could blow off steam by forgetting about her and going out to the pub with him for a pint. But my job pays well, and I easily saved a deposit for this basic top-floor two-bedroom flat in Leith Walk, and I have a minimal mortgage. So I don't need a flatmate. Perhaps I should get one ...

My phone buzzes, and I take a flying leap onto the couch, but it's fallen down the back behind the cushions. Fuck, *fuck!* Panting, I scrabble for it. When I see the message from Florence, a grin spreads across my face.

Who's going to be at this Sunday lunch?

I waste no time in typing a reply.

My parents, my brother and his girlfriend, that's all. Oh and Bitsy, my mum's Bichon Frisé.

I add the last member of the party as a joke, but it's also tactical. Women love cute little balls of fluff, so I'm hoping she'll be more keen to go now. But I wish I hadn't said anything when I receive her reply.

I'd love to but I'm not great with dogs. It could be an issue. Sorry, I just don't want to cause any trouble.

Am I an idiot? Of course not all women like dogs, even cute little balls of fluff. She could be allergic or have a phobia! My thumbs fly over my phone.

Honestly, she's only tiny and very well behaved. We can put her in the laundry if it's a problem? Would really love it if you could be there. You'd be saving me from being the fifth wheel once again (sad emoji)

Face flaming, knowing I'm pushing the second date boundaries to the limit by using emotional blackmail, I wait in anticipation. Minutes tick by, and I consider jerking off just to relieve the tension but can't bring myself to. Finally, after having made a cup of tea, ordering my groceries online, and watching two episodes of a Netflix show, I get a response.

OK, I'll come to Sunday lunch with you, Dr Rhodes. As long as Bitsy doesn't mind going in the laundry. F x

I cheer aloud, do a fist pump, and then reply in a cool, calm, collected manner.

Great. Looking forward to it. D x

CHAPTER 10

Florence | Edinburgh, present day

Call it a blessing, a curse, or a happy accident, but it appears I gave Damian a *partial* memory wipe. I got a bit of shock when he messaged after the flat meeting. He seems to still remember we went on a date but didn't mention anything about the biting, bloodsucking, and fangs—huzzah!

Even more surprising, he invited me to his parents' house for lunch tomorrow, and I debated long and hard with myself about accepting. There's a lot that could go wrong—namely they could find out I'm a vampire if I stuff up. But I said yes. So now that I've made my coffin, I have to lie in it. At least the pesky Bichon Frisé will be out of the way. Dogs tend to sense I'm undead and perceive me as a threat, which is unfortunate as I actually like dogs.

It's also a pity that it's lunch. If it were dinner, I could fly there like I did for our Friday date at The Brief Encounter. But I can't exactly fly around in broad daylight.

***

The next day, just before noon, I step off the bus and start strolling to Damian's parents' house. They live in Blackford, a respectable suburb twenty minutes from the centre of town, with trees and box hedges lining their street. The neatly tended gardens suggest the residents are either retirees or family-oriented professionals. Crime doesn't happen here, and if it does, it's a rare occurrence. I've lived in Edinburgh for long enough now to avoid the hotspots, and this isn't one of them.

Some of the flats we rented when we first moved here in the 1920s would have taken years off my life if I were alive in the normal sense. Thankfully, the shrewd investments we made in British companies after the Depression allowed us to purchase a New Town flat in the 1940s, and they've yielded tidy biannual dividends ever since.

However, we've had to sell up and move quite a few times over the years. When neighbours shoot you suspicious looks because you're not ageing and rumours start, it's time to scour the real estate ads.

Our latest acquisition in Ramsay Garden up by the castle was a steal as it needed renovating, but it was still expensive. Hester suggested buying something cheaper in the Highlands and feeding off animals. Sadie was keen to try it, but I put my foot down. That lifestyle is too primitive for me. I'm a city girl.

Adjusting my sunglasses and fluffing my long dark hair apprehensively, I walk up to the front door and ring the bell. All my spidey senses are on high alert—not just at the thought of seeing Damian again, but because I'm also meeting his family. If Sadie knew I was doing this, she'd have kittens. But there's something that's driving me, and I'm not sure what it is.

Maybe it's because you want a normal life, a little voice whispers in my head. Before I have time to question the validity of that, the door is flung open, and Damian is standing there in all his hot glory. His purple-streaked hair is floppy over his forehead rather than gelled back. The tight white shirt he's wearing stretches across his broad chest and shoulders, its rolled-up sleeves revealing muscular forearms. Black fitted jeans remind me that he's not lacking in the crotch department either. If I could blush, I'd be a red-faced wreck right now.

'Hi, you made it. Come in!' He sounds relieved, and I wonder if he was anxious that I wouldn't show. I could read his thoughts to find out, but now that I know I can, I pull back and stop myself to respect his privacy.

At least he's said the magic words 'come in', so I can step over the threshold. If he hadn't, it would have been awkward. A home is a personal space, so vampires need an invitation to enter. But we can access any public buildings without permission.

As I pass by, I get a good whiff of Damian's aftershave mingled with the sweet scent of his blood. My fangs tingle and start extending.

Shit! I clamp my lips together hard so I don't tackle him to the floor and devour him in his parents' hallway. There's a black-and-white photograph of the Royal Mile in a rainstorm on the wall, and I focus on it intently. Thankfully, the bloodlust gradually subsides.

'Everyone's in the lounge, so let's go through,' Damian says.

I still haven't spoken, and he's looking at me strangely probably because I'm spacing out. And I'm still wearing my oversized Prada sunglasses. Hastily, I take them off and poke them in my handbag. Although I can manage short bursts of direct daylight (up to an hour is fine), too much plays havoc with my retinas, and I have to spend several days in darkness to recover. Sunglasses help. Fortunately, Edinburgh's short daylight hours in winter makes it the perfect gloomy city for our kind to inhabit; the long summer days cause sunburn, so we tend to hibernate then.

Chatter and muted laughter spill out from a lounge situated off the hallway, and I'm afraid that I'm going to say or do something to give myself away. I need to stall.

'Damian.' I touch his shoulder lightly, and he turns to face me. 'Thanks for the invite.'

'You're very welcome. I'm glad you're here.' There's an intensity to his voice, and his eyes are burning into mine. So much for sunlight—*he's* going to damage my retinas. I lick my lips, and his eyes follow the movement. Sensing his strong urge to kiss me, my stomach quivers.

'Are you nervous?' he asks softly.

'A little,' I admit. 'I haven't been to a Sunday lunch in ages.'

Damian slides his warm hand into my cold one and gives it a squeeze, and I relax slightly.

He leans forward and whispers in my ear, 'It's OK, they don't bite', making me huff out a sardonic laugh. 'You have nothing to worry about. They'll love you. And you look beautiful, by the way.'

Damian gazes at me fondly and gives my hand another squeeze, and without warning, I get a sudden flash of what he's thinking. OK, he's fully into me—as in he's seeing me as potential girlfriend material. After. Only. One. Date.

A date that in his mind didn't even involve anything physical. As far as he's concerned, I wasn't drooling over his scrumptious cock or biting into his muscular thigh. He likes what he sees (a quirky goth girl with a penchant for history and Bloody Marys), and he's glad I'm here with him. His master plan to take me back to his after lunch involves more than coffee and chatting too. Wonder of wonders!

I feel a bit bad for eavesdropping, but it's exactly what I need to feel more confident. Standing tall, I lift my chin, and we walk hand in hand into the lounge to greet his parents, who have no inkling Damian just invited a vampire into their home.

CHAPTER 11

Florence | London, 1888

I surface from a deep sleep to discover my room is bathed in shadow. I'm lying fully clothed under the coverlet, and my head feels like it's full of sawdust. All the fear and anxiety I had about living here must have taken its toll, and I dropped off out of exhaustion. But it's strange that I can't remember actually lying down.

Did I meet Charlie?

Or did Dr Dryden show me straight to my room?

It doesn't seem to matter. Any foreboding I may have felt upon arrival has melted away, and my limbs are loose and floppy. I feel nothing but an all-pervading sense of calm.

As I haul myself into a sitting position, I notice my tattered brown suitcase has been placed on top of the wardrobe. I yawn and rub my neck. That was clever of me to unpack before having a nap.

In the hallway, a clock strikes the hour, and I count the chimes: six o'clock. I yawn again and feel so relaxed and sleepy that I almost curl up underneath the covers again.

Then I jerk upright.

Dr Dryden said we were all going to have supper together at six thirty.

You need to get washed and changed, and tidy your hair, girl! It will not do to be late. You are lucky to be even having supper with the doctor and his son! Aunt Ivy's voice sounds in my head and is a stark reminder that I'm a servant of sorts in this house. I can't start taking liberties and acting like I'm Lady Muck.

Dragging myself out of bed, I slide over to the mantel in my stockings and, after a few false starts with the matches, light a couple of candles. A washstand near the window holds a jug of water, and I pour some into the basin and splash my face half-heartedly. The ice-cold slap to my cheeks makes me gasp aloud, but at least it forces me fully awake.

Unbuttoning my dress, I shiver in my stays and drawers and quickly open the wardrobe to take out a fresh dress. They were all laundered before I went away, thanks to Aunt Ivy. So at least I can appear neat and clean at supper, if somewhat dull.

But my half-a-dozen drab dresses are not hanging in the wardrobe. Instead, there are a row of stiff taffeta ones in greens, greys, and blues—muted colours, nothing showy, but they look brand new. I finger a sleeve uncertainly. *Where are my clothes? Whose dresses are these?*

The hallway clock strikes the quarter hour, and unless I want to wear my old ill-fitting dress with its patches and tacked-on hem, I have no choice but to pick one. Taking out the green dress, I slip into it and fumble with the row of side buttons. The dress hugs my figure and doesn't droop or sag in front. It's like it was made for me. I'm taller than average, and my dresses are typically hand-me-downs from much shorter Aunt Ivy. I have to alter and lengthen them with extra material, so to have a dress fit me perfectly like this is wonderful.

All I can conclude is that this is the previous governess's room, she had the same figure as me, and she left her clothes behind. *I can ask Dr Dryden about it at supper*, I think as I dive into my bird's nest, retrieving hairpins, then hastily brushing, coiling, and repinning.

Looking in the mirror when I've finished, it's hard to believe I'm the same woman who walked through the door this morning.

I hope Dr Dryden likes me better now. But as soon as the thought enters my head, I send it packing in disgust. It's one thing to put on someone else's dress, but quite another to be thinking of your new employer removing it.

Daylight has disappeared completely by the time I've put on my boots. Taking one of the candles, I step out onto the landing. Vaguely I recall that Charlie's room is next to mine.

Should I wake him for supper? I creep softly over to his door and put my ear to it, but there's no movement or sound from within. My hand hovers over the doorknob, but a twist of something in my gut makes me decide it's best not to.

I descend the staircase, feeling a little spooked by the pressing darkness. There's not a single lamp lit. Am I here alone? Perhaps Dr Dryden and Charlie went out for supper after all? That's probably the case, so it's grilled cheese on toast for me.

When I reach the end of the staircase, I lift my candle into the black yawning mouth of the hallway and gulp. But there's nothing for it. Hunger is gnawing at my belly like a beast, and I need to eat. Taking a deep breath, I start moving down the hallway towards the kitchen. But as I do, a lamp begins glowing on my left, then another on my right until the entire hallway is bathed in soft yellow light and there are no scary shadows on the wall. The lamps are comforting, but the fact that they're turning on by themselves is not. However, the workings of a house like this is beyond me. Perhaps the gas fittings are playing up.

Passing the dining room door, I stop in my tracks, surprised to hear the low rumble of Dr Dryden's voice. So he is here. Upstairs, the faint chime of the clock striking six thirty reaches my ears. So I forget all about the grilled cheese, knock, and enter.

The dining room table is beautifully laid with white linen, gold-plated cutlery, and an arrangement of pink roses; there's even a lit candelabra. Dr Dryden is in evening dress, his hair slicked back, standing by the table with one hand resting on a chair, staring at his pocket watch. My heart quivers. He looks so handsome and debonair that a sliver of drool starts to edge its way out of my mouth. I suck it back in. I'm starving—for food—that's all.

He looks up as I enter. 'Ah, Miss Hughes, there you are. Do come in and join us.' He pulls out the chair he's holding, and feeling slightly dazed, I walk over and sit at the top of the table.

Only when I'm seated do I realise he's said 'us' and there are three place settings. 'Is Charlie still upstairs, sir?'

Dr Dryden takes the chair on my left and looks over at the far corner of the room, where the candelabra doesn't reach. A figure emerges from the shadows, and my skull prickles in shock. Charlie is not the young boy that I've been imagining and that Aunt Ivy has had me believe. He's a grown man in his early twenties and handsome as sin. Pale face, slicked-back dark hair—a younger version of his father.

'You can't be Charlie,' I whisper.

'I assure you I am. Good evening, Miss Hughes.' He dips

his head slightly, walks over to the other chair, and sits down. My eyes are fixed on him in disbelief as he draws a white linen napkin from its engraved brass holder. He glances at me, and his lips quirk in amusement.

I clench my fists, feeling a sudden flash of anger towards Dr Dryden, who appears to be playing a cruel joke on me. For what purpose, I don't know.

'Would you like some wine?' Dr Dryden gestures to a crystal decanter full of ruby liquid.

I shake my head, too upset to speak.

'Are you all right, Miss Hughes?' he asks gently.

I can't even look at him. The way he was talking on the stairs made me think that Charlie was a sick young boy that needed my care and attention. And from the intense way he's been staring at me ever since my interview, I thought that perhaps he might be considering me as a woman rather than a servant. And then that thought got stronger in my mind, and I started picturing us as a family, that I could be his—

I've got it completely wrong.

Dr Dryden is gazing at me, and I compose myself with an effort. 'I feel like I've been hired under false pretences, sir,' I say stiffly. 'You made me believe your son was 10 years old, but he is not and seems a little mature to need a governess. I'm not sure what is going on, but I think it best that I leave tomorrow morning, first thing.'

Trudging back to Aunt Ivy's with my suitcase is not how I pictured my second day of employment going, but I can't stay here. I can't *adapt* to this odd situation.

'Shall we have supper first and then discuss it?' Dr Dryden lifts the lid on the nearest cloche, and a delicious smell of roast beef hits my nose. Underneath the other cloches are steaming roast potatoes and fresh, hot green peas. My stomach folds in on itself, and I almost groan out loud.

'You like your roast beef well done, I think I remember you saying?'

Losing impetus after my outburst, the sight and smell of food are my undoing. I nod weakly, saliva gathering in my mouth.

Dr Dryden begins to heap meat and vegetables onto my plate and I start eating, albeit suspiciously, watching the pair of them.

'Gravy?' Charlie holds a small white jug aloft, his dark eyes glinting.

I nod and he pours a thin stream of brown liquid over my roast beef. It's perfectly cooked, though a little more rare than well done for my liking.

The men take some slices of roast beef, the pinkest ones, and leave the vegetables.

'You are quite right to be upset, Miss Hughes,' says Dr Dryden, helping himself to the gravy. 'I apologise for not mentioning my son's age at our interview.' He smiles placatingly. 'Charlie has been ill for many years, so he has missed out on a proper education. There is much he doesn't know.'

I swallow my mouthful. 'But what am I supposed to teach him? Not algebra, surely?'

Charlie snorts. 'I like her, Papa. She's funny.'

Dr Dryden shoots him a look. 'As I said, there is much he doesn't know. I am sure there are many subjects in which you could tutor him.'

'And vice versa.' Charlie smirks at me, and my blood runs cold. There's something abnormal about him that I can't put my finger on. And apart from being extremely pale, he doesn't appear to be that ill or weakly.

'Well, that was the appetizer,' mutters Charlie when he's cleared his plate. He dabs at his mouth with his napkin. He studies me as I continue to eat, and I feel like I'm being sized up. For what, I don't know.

'Nice dress you're wearing,' he remarks. 'It looks like Miss Pinkerton's. Or was it Miss Murphy's, Papa?'

'I can't recall,' replies Dr Dryden gruffly.

'Who were they?' I pop the last piece of succulent gravy-smeared beef in my mouth and chew contentedly. It's a pity

I'm leaving as wherever this food came from, I could get used to it. I can't remember the last time I had such a good meal. Actually, I don't think I ever have.

'My last governesses,' says Charlie, dragging my attention back to him.

'Oh. What happened to them?'

He shrugs, and his lips turn up at the corners; they're curiously bloodless like the rest of him.

There's a moment of terse silence, as if he's waiting for something. The hairs on the back of my neck prickle, and time seems to stand still. Something is very wrong.

I start to get up from the table, but before I can, Charlie grabs hold of my arm. 'Not so fast. There's still another course.'

How dare he! I attempt to snatch my arm away, but his grip is like iron. 'Let me go please. I don't want any pudding.' But he doesn't remove his hand.

I look to Dr Dryden for support, but he's sitting there impassively. 'Please tell your son to take his paws off me.'

'It will be easier for you if you don't resist, Miss Hughes,' he says, sounding resigned.

Before I can ask him what he means, Charlie none too gently pushes up the sleeve of my dress, and I stare at him. His eyes are black, obsidian discs; he licks his lips and opens his mouth, baring ivory-white fangs, curved and dripping with some kind of clear liquid. I try to make sense of what I'm seeing, but I can't. But with those teeth, whatever's about to happen to me isn't going to be good.

Panic intensifying, I try to yank my arm away more forcefully. 'Charlie, no! What are you doing? Sir, please, help me! Sir!'

But there's no reply from my employer; he simply sits there, watching me struggle. To my horror, Charlie leans forward and skewers my forearm with his razor-sharp fangs. White-hot pain roars through me, and I scream and thrash against him with all my might. But it's in vain—he's too strong. Charlie licks at the blood pouring from the wound, then begins sucking with long greedy pulls, making horrible grunting noises.

I scream loudly, an animalistic wail, and Charlie growls in annoyance. His free hand whacks at my face with a sickening blow, and my head slams against the table. Then I know nothing more.

Chapter 12

Damian | Edinburgh, present day

'It's fine, dear,' says Mum when I arrive for lunch and I tell her I've invited Florence. 'If she's someone you like, then of course we want to meet her.'

'We usually cook extra anyway. For Bitsy,' Dad chips in.

Mum glances at the empty pillow on the couch, and I cringe, feeling guilty. It's an exceptional circumstance for Bitsy not to be at the family Sunday lunch. She roams around under the table and is slyly slipped bits of roast beef. It's how she got her name. Not only have I disrupted the status quo by inviting a date, but Bitsy has been relegated to the laundry, where she can't do any damage with her tiny teeth.

It is a little strange for Florence to be afraid of a Bichon Frisé, but who am I to judge? I'm deathly afraid of spiders—*all* spiders, even ones that are miniscule.

'Yes, everyone's keen to meet Florence,' remarks my older brother, Andrew. He's ensconced on the couch with his arm around his girlfriend, Amber. They've just moved in together and are basking in a smug, loved-up glow that sets my teeth on edge.

'How did you guys meet?' Andrew shoots me a curious stare, and I know if I say she's a patient, I'm never going to hear the end of it.

'Online,' I reply shiftily.

Andrew winks at me. 'Nice work, bro.'

I ignore him and glance at my watch. It's just gone twelve, and my anxiety is kicking in. *What if she doesn't show? It's going to be excruciating.*

The doorbell rings, and my anxiety eases off slightly. *Thank God.*

'I'll just go and ...' I make a hasty escape to the hallway, pausing to check my hair in the mirror. I quite like the purple streaks left over from the Halloween party I went to with a mate last week. I think it makes me look less boring and slightly alternative. Florence didn't comment, but I saw her eyes flicking to it a few times in the bar.

Again, I try to recall what happened after our date but it's still a blank. From Andrew's wink and remark, he's assumed that I've slept with her, but we haven't actually hooked up. A date at a bar, then Sunday lunch at my parents is like going from zero to a hundred in the relationship timeline. But there's no time to analyse my decision-making. She's here.

I fling open the door.

Florence is wearing big sunglasses and is rocking the Victorian goth vibe to the max. She's wearing a long flowing jacket with tails, a black ruffled dress, and lace-up boots. Her skin is translucent. Deep-purple lips. *My conservative, strait-laced brother in his Lacoste polo shirt is going to lose it.* The thought is quite satisfying.

'Hi, you made it. Come in!'

Florence hesitates for the barest second, then steps inside. As she passes by, I smell her signature floral scent, and I breathe it in deeply.

She still hasn't spoken or taken off her sunglasses and seems mesmerised by the black-and-white photo of Edinburgh that my dad took for his photography class.

'Everyone's in the lounge, so let's go through,' I prompt gently.

She starts at the sound of my voice and removes her sunglasses. *Is she hungover? Did she go on a date with another guy last night and order Bloody Marys?*

'Damian.' She touches my shoulder, and I gaze into her big violet eyes fringed with jet-black lashes (natural, not stuck on). *God, she's gorgeous.*

'Thanks for the invite,' she says.

'You're very welcome. I'm glad you're here.'

She licks her lips, and I feel a strong compulsion to take

her in my arms right here in the hallway and kiss her senseless. But that's probably not a good idea. I haven't even held her hand yet. *Maybe I should do that. What if she pulls away?*

'Are you nervous?' I ask softly.

'A little,' she says, and her small frown pinches my heart. 'I haven't been to a Sunday lunch in ages.'

She looks at me like she needs reassurance. This is my cue. Oh god.

I slide my hand into hers; it's as cold as ice! She must really be freaking out. Giving it a squeeze, I sense her relax slightly. *Yes! It was the right thing to do.* To my elation, she doesn't pull her hand out of mine. Now we're getting somewhere.

'It's OK, they don't bite,' I say, making her chuckle. 'You have nothing to worry about. They'll love you. And you look beautiful, by the way.'

Time to shut up now, Damian. But I can't help it, I like her. I'm sure it's written all over my face anyway. Juliana always said I wore my heart on my sleeve. But I don't want to think about her now; this is me moving on ...

Florence and I walk into the lounge hand in hand to greet my family. Hopefully, this will be our first Sunday lunch of many.

***

The dining table seats six, so there's usually an empty chair beside me, but not today. Florence deciding to come for lunch is part of the reason why I'm so into her. She didn't have to. She could have made some lame excuse to get out of it. But whether she agreed to it because she felt obligated or because she likes me, I can't tell. She's one of those inscrutable types. Yet she *did* hold my hand and only dropped it when Mum shooed us through to the dining room, so I'm encouraged by that.

Andrew is being smarmily polite to Florence but openly gawking at her, which is making me want to laugh. Amber isn't any better—steadily eating her meal and half listening to Andrew's prattle in her right ear, but with her eyes roving over Florence. Dad, at the head of the table, is on his best behaviour (namely not burping). To give Florence credit, she's handling it well. Either she's blithely unaware of the attention, or she's used to it and chooses to ignore it.

Mum is the only one who's acting passably normal. She's asking the usual sorts of questions you'd expect from a stranger, and I'm finding out things without having to pry. Excellent. So far, Mum has discovered where Florence lives (Ramsay Garden in the Old Town), her flatmates' names (Sadie and Hester), and that she's writing a book.

'What's that about?' I ask curiously, wondering why Florence didn't mention it at the bar. Perhaps I didn't ask the right questions. Then again, my mum is quite astute. She's an anthropology professor who lectures at Edinburgh University and is used to analysing whole societies based on the barest of evidence.

'It's a memoir,' says Florence after a reluctant pause.

'Aren't you a little young to write a memoir?' Amber says, sounding amused.

'I'm an old soul,' replies Florence. There's a flinty edge to her tone, and I glance up from my meal to see Amber isn't smiling anymore.

'You don't have to be old in years to have life experience,' I tell her. 'Some people pack a lot in before they're even 30.'

'Exactly,' says Florence. But she doesn't elaborate on what her life experiences are or explain why they would merit writing a book.

'Are you going to try and get a publisher for it?' asks Mum. 'That would be exciting.'

'Maybe. When it's finished.' I can tell by her flat tone that she's sorry she mentioned it.

'What's your surname, Florence?' asks Dad, studying her.

'Hughes,' she replies steadily.

He flattens his lips and frowns. 'You look really familiar to me, but I can't put my finger on it. You're not an actor, are you? Theatre?'

Florence shakes her head and laughs a little. 'No, that's my flatmate Hester's side gig. She's into amateur dramatics.'

Dad! For God's sake, leave her alone. I scowl and shake my head at him.

'Oh well, I'm sure it will come to me. I've got a good memory for faces.'

'It's all those sudokus, darling,' says Mum fondly.

He drops it, thank goodness as it's getting embarrassing. But Florence doesn't seem to mind, outwardly anyway.

'Does anyone want any more? There's some beef left. Florence? You haven't eaten much.'

Mum hands her the plate before she can say no. 'OK, thank you.'

Florence takes a slice. I notice she's pushed what few vegetables she had to the side. Then again, so have my dad and I as it's Brussels sprouts, and we hate them.

Looks like Bitsy's going to be getting a vegetarian supper, I think.

Speaking of which, I can hear distant whining and growling. She emits a volley of sharp barks, and Florence jerks next to me.

'Don't worry,' I say. 'She's in the laundry. I put her there myself.'

Florence gives me a grateful smile.

Bitsy yaps again, and Mum says, 'Strange, she never usually barks. She must be hungry.'

Mum loads some scraps of beef onto a small plate and goes off to feed her. But a few moments later, there's the sound of scampering paws, and there she is in the doorway: a tiny ball of white fluff with black beady eyes—Mum's third child. She must have evaded her and run out to see everyone.

'Hello, Bitsy. Oh, you're so cute! I definitely think we should get a Bichon Frisé, Andy,' says Amber.

'Over my dead body,' mutters my brother.

'But what's wrong with her?'

Amber's right—Bitsy is acting strangely, standing stock-still and trembling. She takes a step forward, plants her little feet, and lets out a volley of short sharp barks, then runs backwards and forwards in the doorway, growling menacingly, which is quite a feat for a Bichon Frisé.

We all stare in fascination, apart from Florence, who is cowering against me. I put my arm around her. 'It's OK, she sometimes goes a little nuts after she's been shut away.'

Mum comes running in.

'Bitsy! Stop that!'

She tries to grab her, but Bitsy scoots under the table.

Seconds later, Florence lets out a piercing scream. I look down and can't believe my eyes. Bitsy, who would never hurt a fly, has sunk her teeth into Florence's leg and is snarling like a savage beast.

Chapter 13

Florence | Edinburgh, present day

Damian springs into action. He pries the crazed little dog's jaw open, wrestles her off my leg, and whisks me into the family bathroom. I'm placed on the toilet seat lid, which has a fluffy peach cover, and my leg is propped on the edge of the bath.

'My hero,' I whisper as I lean back against the cistern, trying to keep a straight face as he kneels beside me, inspecting the damage. 'Thank you for saving me. My leg was in danger of being gnawed off.'

He peers at my shin worriedly, and I suppose it looks a bit gruesome, but I consider it a minor flesh wound. I've had worse.

'Now you see why I don't like dogs,' I joke, trying to make him laugh. But Damian's still too concerned about me to crack a smile. He rootles through the vanity, looking for the first aid kit, and swears under his breath when he finds it.

'There's no fucking antiseptic wipes, only Savlon.'

'Just bung a plaster on it, honestly.'

Anxiety and misery are rolling off him in waves, and I feel bad for him. After a sneak peek into his thoughts, I discover he's stressing madly because he thinks I'm not going to like him after this.

'Damian.' I grasp his shoulder to reassure him that I'm perfectly OK. He stops fussing with the kit and looks at me.

'What?'

'I'm fine. It's not life-threatening. It's going to take a lot more than a tiny fluff ball to finish me off.' *Or keep me away from you.*

He frowns, unconvinced.

'Honestly, it looks worse than it is. Dogs always go for me. I must have been a cat in a former life.'

He smiles briefly at my joke, but then his face is back to serious mode.

'I'll do what I can for now,' he says. 'But you should make an appointment with your doctor to get it checked out—you might need antibiotics or a tetanus shot.'

'You can give me an injection anytime, Dr Rhodes,' I say huskily and get a half-hearted chuckle (finally). I stroke the back of his neck, attempting to soothe him as he washes away the blood, dabs Savlon gently on the wound, and opens a packet of plasters.

I'm quite enjoying him looking after me, and if my history is anything to go by, I do have a thing for hot doctors.

Damian carefully places a large beige plaster over the wound, and not a minute too soon, as the edges are already starting to knit together.

I move my hand up the back of his head, playing with the ends of his hair. He shudders, probably because my hand is cold.

'All done.' He pats my bare knee with his warm hand, and my pale skin tingles. 'Is it sore?'

I shake my head, trying not to get too excited from his touch.

'We'll keep an eye on it.'

I nod. 'Thanks, Doc. Do I get a lollipop now?'

He huffs a laugh. 'I think we missed dessert ...'

'Oh?'

He turns and holds my eyes with his as my fingers trace the soft spot between his ear and his cheek.

'But maybe a kiss would help?' he murmurs.

A slow wave of desire rolls through my body.

'Yes, I think it would definitely help with the healing process.'

His mouth curves in approval, and his lovely lips inch towards mine. Mmm, I've been looking forward to snogging Dr Rhodes ever since our liaison in my bedroom.

We're just about to kiss when there's a sharp knock on the door.

'Everything all right in there?' calls Andrew. 'You're not amputating her leg, are you?'

Damian jerks back, and the first aid kit goes flying into the bath. He throws me a look of apology, hastily gets to his feet, and unlocks the door.

Andrew pokes his head in and grins when he sees Damian looking flustered, as if he knows he interrupted an intimate moment and is congratulating himself on his good timing. I narrow my eyes and barely stop myself from growling. It was pretty *bad* timing as far as I'm concerned, even if Damian's parents' bathroom isn't exactly the most romantic of venues for a first kiss.

'How's the patient?' asks Andrew, staring at my plastered shin. I pull down my dress to stop him from gawping.

'She'll live,' I say. 'Thanks to your brother's handiwork.' I lift my leg down from the bath, and Damian's instantly by my side.

'Take it easy,' he urges, putting an arm around my waist and helping me to my feet.

Andrew smirks.

We walk down the hallway behind him to the lounge, and I sense Damian is torn about what to do next.

'Do you want to come back to mine?' he whispers in my ear. 'I could make you a hot chocolate and look after you properly.'

I hesitate, sorely tempted by that offer. Not the hot chocolate so much, but him looking after me—and exploring that almost kiss. Even just snuggling with him would be divine. If I *was* a cat in a former life, Damian would most definitely be my catnip.

But I'm not sure it's a good idea.

After the dog episode, I need to lie low, possibly distance myself from him and his family. His father was asking a lot of questions.

'I should probably go home, get a blood transfusion or something.'

I say it as a joke but I'm serious. Ingesting roast beef is fine as it gets broken down and absorbed into my body over a period of days, but it's not the nourishment I crave.

'Yeah, all right then.' He sounds disappointed, and I don't want to be parted from him just yet either.

I think quickly.

Hester is out, but Sadie and Elliott are at the flat. Hopefully, Sadie is distracted enough by Elliott not to sense anything happening downstairs.

'What about if you escort me home?' I say, and Damian presses a kiss to my temple.

'Perfect.'

***

'Does your leg hurt?'

It's the fifth time Damian's asked me that, and if he doesn't quit it soon, I'm going to throttle him.

We're on the top floor of the bus heading back to the Old Town, and I'm regretting my decision to allow him to escort me home. Maybe I should say I'm in agony so he'll be satisfied that I'm normal, but that would be lying.

'No, it doesn't hurt. You should probably stop asking me as my answer isn't going to change anytime in the next hour.' I keep my tone light, but firm.

But Damian frowns. 'That's so weird. Bitsy sank her teeth quite deeply into your flesh. I had to practically force her jaw open to make her let go, and you feel *nothing*?'

My nonbitten leg starts jiggling nervously as I sense he's seriously starting to question why I'm not in pain.

'Unless you're in shock,' he continues. 'Maybe I should take your pulse.'

He reaches for my wrist, and I move my arm away hastily.

'I have an extremely high pain threshold. It's a thing,' I tell him, and to my relief, he nods.

'I've come across a few people like that at work. I once gave a guy a root canal without anaesthetic, and he didn't even blink.'

'Yes, I can relate. I've never had a root canal, but I know

I could probably handle one without needing drugs.'

Damian raises an eyebrow and looks impressed.

The fact that he deals with teeth for his job is probably why he's more curious than most people about pain thresholds. I need to get him off the subject.

'Ah, your family was really nice about it. I hope Bitsy doesn't get reprimanded too much.'

'I wouldn't worry. She'll be mollycoddled for the next week by Mum.'

Before we left, his mum apologised profusely to me. She said the attack happened because Damian shut her in the laundry and Bitsy was upset that she was excluded from the lunch.

'I thought it was a little unfair to blame you, though. If it was anyone's fault, it's mine. You were only trying to make me feel comfortable.'

Damian shrugs offhandedly. 'Nah, you were the victim. It's OK, I'll cry about it later. I'm used to being the scapegoat,' he says, not sounding too worried. 'Bitsy is nuts anyway.'

But Bitsy isn't nuts. I knew she would act like that. Random canine attacks are standard for me, especially as Edinburgh is so dog-friendly. I once had a chihuahua go for me on a bus—it wasn't pretty.

I bite my lip and say nothing because I can't tell him the truth. He'd freak out and get off at the next bus stop.

Fortunately, there aren't any dogs on board at the moment—two canine attacks in one day would really make Damian start wondering about me.

He strokes the back of my hand, and I relax, letting him. 'Your hands are always so cold,' he murmurs, and I tense up again.

'I have bad circulation. It's hereditary.'

Hmm, perhaps dating someone in the medical profession isn't so wise after all? But it's too late now. I can't seem to extricate myself from this deepening attraction, and I'm not sure I want to. Damian is now attempting to warm my hands by chafing them in his own larger ones. He doesn't try any more pulse taking, to my relief.

It's actually pretty sweet. *He's* sweet. And kind. The fact that he's also gorgeous is giving him several extra brownie points.

'Is this helping at all?'

'Possibly. You might need to keep going for a bit longer, though,' I say, watching his muscular forearms flex as he rubs my cold pale hands briskly. *They're never going to warm up, but I could get used to this ...*

CHAPTER 14

Florence | London, 1888

Ladybird, ladybird,
Fly away home,
Your house is on fire,
And your children are gone.

The nursery rhyme infiltrates my mind, and I want it to cease. Yet it's relentless, as if the person is singing it to soothe me—or to make me forget.

My right arm throbs, and my mouth is parched.

'Water,' I croak.

The singing stops, and a figure emerges from a dark corner and sits on the side of the bed. My head is lifted, and a cup placed to my lips. The liquid that fills my mouth isn't water, yet it tastes delicious, and I gulp it down.

After finishing, I'm lowered back to the pillow, and Dr Dryden comes into focus. My eyes rove over him, drinking in his handsome face greedily.

My master.

A strange and slightly painful prickling sensation rushes over my skin, making me gasp. Then it sinks through my flesh and courses through my entire body. *I must have a fever—my veins are on fire! And why am I thinking of Dr Dryden as my master? How embarrassing. Thank God I didn't say it out loud.*

I catch sight of a cream bandage wound around my arm almost up to the elbow, which shocks me even further.

'Wha-what happened?' I attempt to sit up, and the room tilts alarmingly.

'Hush now. Just lie still and rest,' Dr Dryden says. His deep voice is silky smooth, and I'm comforted by the sound of it.

He presses me back into the pillow, and I sink willingly. There's a brief touch of cool fingers on my hot skin as he smooths back a strand of hair from my forehead.

'Why is my arm bandaged?' I ask him, struggling to remember.

'You had an accident, Florence.' The way he says my name, like he's savouring it on his tongue, makes me shiver. 'In the kitchen. You were cutting slices of cheese for your supper, and the knife must have slipped. I found you on the floor ... bleeding.'

A hazy memory surfaces and then dissipates.

'Bleeding? Oh.' I lick my lips, tasting the remnants of the

drink he gave me, and look at my arm. I wiggle my fingers. My hand still works, thank goodness. But I can feel the wound pulsating. *I must have cut it very badly.* 'What a clumsy klutz. Did you look after me? Thank you.'

His wintry hand returns to my forehead, gently stroking, and it feels so blissfully refreshing that a small whimper escapes before I can stop it.

The corner of Dr Dryden's mouth lifts slightly. He trails a finger down the side of my cheek and under my chin, tickling it like I'm a cat. A pleasant feeling pricks between my legs, causing my hips to squirm. I nuzzle into his hand, almost purring in pleasure, which shocks me. *What am I doing?*

'You gave us quite a scare,' he says softly, his thumb caressing my lower lip.

A strong urge to suck and bite his thumb arises, which I push aside immediately. *What would he think?*

I refocus on his face with difficulty.

'Us?'

'Yes, me and Charlie.'

Charlie was there? I try my hardest, but I can't remember him at all. I'm so confused, and Dr Dryden lightly stroking along my jawline isn't helping.

'Did I meet him?'

'Briefly.' His voice is distracted and his eyes, now a

darker shade of brown, are locked on my throat. He presses his fingers against my neck, feeling for my pulse.

He must be doing another health examination to determine how I am, I think. *I must have lost a lot of blood from cutting myself ...*

His cold fingers are now tracing the column of my throat and dancing lightly along the neckline of my chemise.

Oh!

Does he need to examine my chest? But the injury is on my arm ...

The feeling between my legs intensifies as his fingers slide underneath the material and then lower down, drawing small circles on the fleshy tops of my breasts. His fingers brush one of my nipples, and I moan softly, arching my back as a jolt of pleasure infuses my body.

Dr Dryden glances quickly at the door as if to reassure himself it's closed and leans in closer. 'Do you like that, Florence?' he murmurs. His icy fingers flick gently at my hard nipple, and white lightning strikes between my thighs.

'Oh *yes*, please keep doing it, Master,' I say and groan in shame. What is the matter with me? I'm obviously not in my right mind due to blood loss. Aunt Ivy would be horrified. But Aunt Ivy isn't here, *and it feels so good* ... I groan again as his hand reaches down to cup my breast.

'Shall I stop?' Dr Dryden enquires, fingers pausing.

I shake my head quickly. There's an eyebrow arch of approval, and he quickly undoes the tie of my chemise. I sigh as he pulls it down to expose my white breasts and rosy-pink buds. He gazes in reverential silence, then begins gently kneading them in his glacial hands, pinching my stiff nipples between his fingers while I squirm in pleasure. Dr Dryden's face is impassive as he touches me, but I sense his excitement, taut like a wire within him.

'You're a very beautiful girl, Florence,' he says, his voice wavering slightly, as he continues to toy with my tender peaks. My face is burning that I'm half naked and writhing under his watchful gaze. But I'm hot and yearning for his touch, and I can't seem to control myself.

He's making me lose my mind.

Moisture drips from between my thighs and soaks the bedsheets. My arousal scents the air, and his nostrils flare. I know he wants me like I want him—I can sense it keenly.

Desperately seeking relief, I rip my chemise down the middle so I'm completely naked, but I don't care. I grab one of his large elegant hands off my breast and move it lower, towards my sex, shivering in anticipation.

He gives a low chuckle and says, 'Naughty girl,' but doesn't pull away. Yet his hand, the one I'm currently guiding between my legs, trembles slightly. His eyes drop to my neck again, and he licks his lips.

'Damn you, Charlie,' he says softly. It's so quiet I almost miss it, but my hearing has become surprisingly sensitive.

He must be having second thoughts about interfering with his son's governess, but it's a bit late for that.

I drive his hand between my legs and moan as his fingers stroke my wetness while his other hand runs over my breasts, tugging lightly on my nipples.

'Yes, *yes*,' I groan and undulate my hips to gain more friction from his stroking fingers. There's an insatiable pulsing need between my thighs—and only he can relieve it.

But Dr Dryden suddenly stops stroking me and cups my entire sex firmly, as if to steel himself not to dip his fingers between my damp folds. *What is he doing?* I fume. *He needs to touch me properly.* Frustrated, I open my thighs wide and rub against his hand wantonly, seeking my pleasure and not caring a jot about propriety.

'My master,' I moan. 'My *lord*.'

Suddenly, there's a growl, a flash of white teeth, a whirl of a black jacket.

And I'm alone in the room, wild-eyed and unsatiated. I let out a mournful howl—loud enough to wake the dead.

CHAPTER 15

Damian | Edinburgh, present day

Florence and I walk up The Mound heading towards Ramsay Garden. It feels natural that we're holding hands, after my attempts to warm hers up. But they're still as frosty as ever despite my concerted efforts. I could tell Florence thought it was amusing, but I might do some research on that. What with the high pain threshold and bad circulation, her physiology is starting to interest me as much as her personality.

My degree is in dentistry, but I initially had plans to be a surgeon as I find human anatomy fascinating. I used to have a much more *morbid* interest in it. A knee-jerk reaction to what happened with Juliana, I suppose. I haven't analysed it too deeply. But I don't think there's anything wrong with wanting to take care of your loved ones ...

'This way, dreamy. It's up the hill.' Florence tugs on my hand, and I'm roused from my thoughts. As we start to climb higher, the historic Ramsay Garden apartments come into view. Their red-and-white exteriors, towers, and turrets stand out against the skyline. It's pretty cool that Florence lives in one of them. Looking back, the Georgian buildings of New Town are spread out below; in front is the honey-coloured National Gallery, and next to it, the blackened Gothic spire of Scott Monument. The sound of distant bagpipes floats on the breeze.

'How long have you lived up here?' I ask conversationally.

'About seven years,' Florence replies.

That means she must've been living here since she was 20. Her date of birth was on her dental records, and she's 27, two years younger than me. Regardless of that, her skin is smooth and clear without a wrinkle. Still it's no indication of a woman's age these days as she could be using Botox. I'm not judging.

I stop for a breather and to peer through the wrought-iron gate at the neatly maintained private back gardens.

'Do you rent, or does one of your flatmates own the apartment?' I enquire.

'We own it between us,' she says after a pause.

'Oh.' *Interesting arrangement.*

'Was it difficult to get financing?' I ask, digging for more information in a roundabout way.

'No, we bought it outright.'

My eyebrows rise at that. Wow. Ramsay Garden is right

next to the Royal Mile and a stone's throw from the castle, it's a prime location. Did she receive an inheritance, or did her family win lotto? Or does she secretly own a unicorn start-up?

I glance at her curiously, but I can't see her eyes. She's wearing those infernal sunglasses, even though the sky is a dull grey. Yet from the set of her plum lips, I gather she doesn't want me to ask her any more questions.

Rein it in, Rhodes. After what happened with Bitsy, you're lucky she let you walk her to her flat.

What's going to happen when we get there, I have no idea.

A cup of tea?

Polite conversation?

Making out?

My expectations are low. At this stage, I'd settle for a cup of tea and a chat.

We continue walking up the winding cobblestone road until Florence stops by a black front door with a lion's head knocker and turns to face me.

'Thanks for seeing me home after the vicious Bichon Frisé attack, Damian, and administering first aid, of course. I appreciate it.' She gives me a small smile.

I smile back. 'Anytime.'

'This is my private entrance. That's the main door up

there.' She gestures with a tilt of her head to the curving flight of stairs above us in case I'm wondering.

I nod, checking out the shiny red door at the top.

Florence inserts her key in the lock. There's no invitation to join her.

I'm careful not to let the disappointment show on my face. Looks like I'm spending the rest of the afternoon by myself, pouring my own tea and fantasising about the making out. But it's more than that. I wanted to hang out with her. Get to know her better. What if she doesn't want to see me again after this? Is her lovely hair, flowing in glossy waves halfway down her back, the last glimpse I'll ever have of her?

For a second, I can't breathe. Then self-protection kicks in.

'Well, thanks for coming over for lunch, Florence,' I say in my professional dentist voice. 'Again, I'm sorry about the dog incident, and I do urge you to go to your doctor to get it checked out.' I shove a hand in my jacket pocket, taking out my gloves in preparation for the walk back to Leith. Catching the bus will just remind me of us holding hands.

Florence glances back over her shoulder at me.

'Aren't you coming in?' she asks, sounding faintly surprised.

I instantly drop the formal facade.

'Oh, I thought you might want to rest ...'

Florence lowers her sunglasses an inch and pierces me with her violet eyes. 'Well, I was going to have a lie-down. You're welcome to join me if you're feeling tired.'

My cock springs to life in my jeans. We are on the same page after all.

***

Florence's bedroom takes me by surprise. Has she done some kind of Victorian interior design course? I'm impressed at her dedication to historical accuracy. I feel like I've stepped back into the nineteenth century. But it's also bloody freezing in here, and my desire for hot sex is fading fast since I don't fancy getting naked.

'Is the central heating not on?' I ask, shivering even though I'm bundled up in my winter coat.

Florence looks at me with an inscrutable expression and shakes her head. 'No, sorry. My flatmate Sadie is a stickler for keeping it off during the day.'

'Right.'

She opens her mouth slightly as if to explain further but then closes it again. But I get it. Sadie is one of *those* flatmates, and she doesn't want a confrontation with her.

Oh well, I'm sure we can keep each other warm under

the bedcovers ...

Florence begins picking up books and straightening various objects around the room and seems nervous all of a sudden. Like now that she's invited me in, she's not quite sure what to do with me. Her provocative manner has disappeared, and she seems younger somehow, inexperienced.

'Hey.' I grab her hand as she waltzes past me for the third time, clutching a vase, apologising for the room's disarray. 'Your bedroom is fine.'

'Really?'

'Yeah, it's cool. But if you *do* want to have a lie-down, we should probably get into bed at some point,' I say, attempting to lighten the mood. 'But only if you want to. And nothing needs to happen.' I add, 'You know ... sexually.'

The word hangs in the frigid air between us. She doesn't say anything. Her violet eyes bore into mine as if she's considering that statement, and I blush. *Oh god, I'm so bad with this stuff!*

Fortunately, Florence nods slowly in agreement. 'OK.'

She sits on the side of the bed and starts unlacing her boots, and I follow suit with my trainers but remain upright, leaning against the wall. However, I've made tight knots in my shoelaces as I'm terrible at tying them and they always come undone. I struggle to unpick the knots and end up hopping and yanking my trainers off my feet, leaving the laces tied. I chuck them off to the side by the wall, where they land in a jumble. How I'm going to get them back on my feet, I don't know.

Florence's mouth twists, watching the performance. I'm glad my antics amuse her. She flips back the red satin bedcover to expose white silk sheets beneath. Fancy!

'Should I slip into something more comfortable perhaps?' Her hand hovers at the neckline of her black blouse and fiddles with one of the pearl buttons. The seductive way she's looking at me is causing my groin to stir. She seems older now; the temptress is back.

'All right,' I say eagerly. 'I mean, uh, sure, that sounds like a good idea.'

Florence huffs a laugh as if she knows exactly what I'm visualising in my mind. Then again, I'm a guy—it's not like I'm that hard to figure out.

She disappears behind the wooden changing screen in front of the armoir. Its white panels are decorated with painted flowers and naked cherubs. Moments later, there's the rustling of material.

I sit on the edge of the bed, looking around the room, absorbing the details properly. It's all so old-fashioned. The leatherbound books, the sideboard with a crystal decanter of port, the antique clock ticking away on the mantelpiece. A strong feeling of déjà vu washes over me, like I've seen all this before. That I was even offered a glass of port. But how could I have? This is the first time I've set foot in here. I shake my head, feeling confused.

Florence's dress is flung over the top of the screen and some kind of undergarment. A wooden drawer opens, and there's a rummaging sound.

I feel like a sleazy gentleman in a lady's boudoir.

'Hop into bed if you like.' Florence's voice floats out from behind the screen. 'I won't be a minute.'

I thought 'slip into something more comfortable' was a euphemism for sexy underwear, but when Florence appears in a floor-length white cotton nightgown with ruffles at the wrists, it suddenly strikes me that she might actually be serious about napping.

Unfortunately, by this time, I've taken off my coat, jeans, and shirt and am lying in my boxer briefs underneath the silk sheets. Now I realise I've been way too eager, and my previous assertion that 'nothing needs to happen' is going to look like a massive fib. But it's too late now; she's sliding into bed next to me. Florence props her head on her elbow.

'Are you feeling a bit warmer now?' she asks.

'Well, not really.'

She peeks under the covers and giggles. 'Why, Dr

Rhodes, you seem to have lost your clothes.'

'And you seem to have gained some different ones,' I say, eyeing the complicated ties on the front of her nightgown and wondering how they undo. This isn't how I envisioned us getting together at all.

I jerk as the tip of Florence's icy finger touches my shoulder and traces the outline of the *J* entwined with a thorny rose. *Crap, I forgot about my tattoo.* Her fingernail circles it.

'What's the significance of this?' she asks.

'It's ...' I swallow. But my throat closes up, and for a moment, I can't speak. Florence looks at me curiously, completely unaware of the emotions unleashing inside me. Sweat breaks out on my forehead. She really *shouldn't* have asked, but she deserves to know what she's signing up for if she gets involved with me. *I want to tell her.*

'It's my girlfriend's initial. She ... she died two years ago,' I choke out.

Chapter 16

Florence | Edinburgh, present day

Holy shit. I gaze at the *J* rose tattoo and don't say anything. Damian's breathing is erratic, and he looks at me wide-eyed, like he's about to lose it. OK, this is a bad wound, something that he keeps tightly locked away and why I haven't picked up on it from his thoughts. But it seems he's also suffering from PTSD. I've been through two world wars, so I know a bit about the effects of shell shock.

I rub his forearm to let him know I'm not going anywhere. That he's in a safe space. 'Hey, what happened? You can tell me,' I say in a low soothing voice.

Damian stares at me, his cheeks red and his forehead sweaty. 'You want to hear about Juliana?' He sounds amazed, like he's expecting me to kick him out of bed.

I nod. 'She's part of your history—of course I want to hear about her.' *And I'm not squeamish about death since I've been a vampire for over a century ...*

The look of utter relief on Damian's face is enough to melt my long dormant heart. Oh, the poor wee mite! I rearrange the white goose-feather bed pillows, plumping them up behind his head so he's comfortable. I take his hand in mine and wait for him to begin.

'It ... it was a car accident,' he says shakily, and I squeeze his fingers.

'Go on.'

He closes his eyes, and the words flow out of him in a fast moving stream, as if he wants to get it over with.

'Three of us ... camping trip ... My friend Jake, he'd been drinking ... driving too fast ... clipped an oncoming car ... It rolled ... Juliana in front ... n-not wearing a seat belt ... Ambulance took ages ... We were in the middle of nowhere ... She lost too much b-blood ... They said her death was p-preventable if we'd been nearer a town ...'

'I'm so sorry,' I murmur. 'Did anyone else ...? Your friend?'

'Jake was fine apart from some cuts and bruises,' replies Damian flatly, and I get the sense he and Jake aren't friends anymore. I take a quick peek into his thoughts. Yep, he's never forgiven Jake and hopes he burns in hell. Whoa.

'I could have saved her, but I didn't know how,' Damian continues. 'I was in dental school, studying teeth, not human anatomy. I could do basic CPR, but I was clueless about serious injuries. If I'd been studying medicine, I could have done something ... tried something ...' He clenches his fists lying on top of the bedcover, and his knuckles turn white.

'It wasn't your fault, Damian,' I say gently.

'Afterwards, I tried to retrain as a doctor. But I kept failing—it was the grief, I suppose,' he goes on as if I haven't spoken. 'I couldn't handle the stress, and I balked when we had to dissect corpses. Every time, I'd get stuck. It felt like I was reliving her death all over again. I failed one time too many, and they kicked me out. So I went back to dentistry and finished my course. But I vowed to learn everything I could in case it happened again, to anyone. If I'd had more knowledge, I could have kept her stable before the ambulance arrived. I've done so much medical research since it happened that I could probably perform basic surgery on the roadside.' He gives a short bitter laugh.

Now I know why he was so anxious about Bitsy biting me. But compared to some of the other more dramatic ways I could go, death by Bichon Frisé would be a tad embarrassing ...

'And how has it affected your personal life? If you don't mind me asking. Have you had a girlfriend since?' I attempt to sound neutral like I'm a therapist, but I'm keen to hear the answer.

He shrugs. 'No. I've dated a bit here and there, but I guess I haven't wanted to get close to anyone ... in case they

... you know ... like Juliana.'

I nod. 'Understandable. But you can't think like that. Otherwise, you'll wake up one day and realise you've wasted the best years of your life. You're hot and a nice person. You deserve to be happy.'

I'm not just giving him compliments because I want him to be happy with me. He *really* doesn't deserve the emotional and mental anguish he's torturing himself with. If anyone should be feeling guilty about their past misdeeds, it should be me, not him.

Damian inclines his head slightly. 'You think I'm hot?'

I smile to myself. Of course he's focused on that part of my pep talk! 'Smoking.' I lean in to give him a light peck on the cheek, but he turns his head and presses his lips hard against mine. We kiss for a brief moment, and it's lovely.

But then he pulls away, shaking like a leaf, burying his face in his hands. 'I'm sorry,' he whispers. 'I just get these stupid panic attacks.'

I put my arm around his shoulders and hold him close to me, then get a bit worried that he won't feel me breathing and wonder why. Especially if he's done a lot of medical research. I drop my arm and inch away from his body slightly but don't want him to feel like I'm rejecting him. 'Would a cup of tea help perhaps?'

He nods and takes a shaky breath. 'Yeah, that would be

great. Thanks. And thanks for listening.'

'Not a problem. How do you take it?'

'White with one sugar.' Damian smiles weakly and burrows down into the soft pillows—not before I catch a glimpse of his red watery eyes, though.

Yikes. Hopefully, it did help him to talk about his girlfriend. I'm not usually sought out by either of my flatmates for deep and meaningful conversations, so hopefully, I did OK.

Carefully, I tuck the covers around him and retreat from my lair. Discombobulated, I head upstairs, surprised that I'm feeling protective and maternal towards Damian right now. I still want to fuck him and suck his blood, but alongside that is a strong urge to comfort and take care of him—it's a new feeling for me.

***

Sadie is boiling the kettle when I reach the kitchen. Good timing!

'Hello, witch,' she says, sensing me in the doorway.

'Don't call me that,' I say automatically, watching as she pours hot water into a tartan mug. Luckily, we have tea and coffee for Elliott, or it would be hot water or blood on offer for Damian. Not for the first time I realise how weird this set-up is: three female vampires living together and one of them involved with a thrall who keeps us supplied in blood bags.

I sigh and perch on a bar stool, waiting for Sadie to finish. She draws a sharp knife lightly across her wrist, and blood drips into the coffee as she stirs it. Ah, OK, he must need 'revitalising'.

'Is Elliott upstairs?'

'No, in the lounge. We got a bit carried away ... on the couch. I'll clean it.'

I screw up my nose. 'Hester and I sit on that couch. Couldn't you have gone up to your room?'

'Well, when the mood takes you. But now I know why it did.' She rubs at the cut on her wrist distractedly, which has all but disappeared, then folds her arms, eyeing my nightgown. 'He's downstairs, isn't he? That horny dentist of yours. I thought I could sense arousal. It set me off.'

'Perhaps he was horny when we arrived, but he's not now. He's upset. His girlfriend died. Two years ago. He opened up to me about it. I'm making him a cup of tea. To comfort him.'

'Oh, I see.' Sadie's lip curls, showing a glimpse of fang, and she turns and reaches for a packet of Bourbon Creams from the cupboard. Biscuits as well! They must have had a good session for Elliott to be needing the works. She's comforting him just as much as I am Damian. She's *such* a hypocrite.

'Have we still got that hot-water bottle of Elliott's?'

Sadie gestures at the drawer below my knee with her chin. 'I think it's in there.'

I open the drawer and find the hot-water bottle with its pink knitted cover under a pile of old *Vogue* magazines.

Sadie clicks her tongue. 'So you've got a half-naked dentist in your bed who hasn't realised exactly what you are yet. And you're worried that once he does, he's going to freak out despite you playing psychoanalyst and being all *comforting*—as if that's going to make a difference.'

'Thanks, Miss Mind Reader. But I really don't need your opinion about it,' I say through gritted teeth. 'And his name is *Damian*.'

'Floss, I'm just reminding you that fraternising with humans never ends well. You know you need to break it off,' she says, her voice softening.

'Damian's different,' I say stubbornly, filling the hot-water bottle. 'Besides, you've got Elliott. You don't understand what it's like.'

Sadie walks over to the door with the mug of revitalising coffee in one hand and the packet of Bourbon Creams in the other.

'Floss,' she says, sounding impatient. I shake my head

and put my hands over my ears, but her voice penetrates my mind anyway, and I can't stop it.

I do understand what it's like. I'm 130 years older than you, and I was alone for most of those before we met. I know it's difficult. But the longer you leave it, the harder it's going to be. You know I'm right—

I interrupt her. *I didn't ask for this. I didn't ask Alexander to turn me!* I clutch the hot-water bottle to my chest. But I'm impervious to heat, so it doesn't comfort me.

I know you didn't. But you need to grow up. Dragging a human into our world is irresponsible when you know what Alexander could do to him ...

Sadie gives me a grave look and exits to tend to her weak thrall, leaving me slumped against the kitchen counter, hurt and angry at her lack of compassion for my situation. *Sanctimonious bitch*, I think.

I heard that, Floss. Go and see to your dentist. And don't be mad at me. I'm just keeping it real. We can discuss it more later if you need to.

Oops, I forgot she was only in the lounge.

I head downstairs to get out of her range, slightly mollified, but still justifiably upset. Sadie's got a point, but she's not always right. Yes, it's risky to get involved with a human, but I trust that Hester's got my back when it comes to shielding me. She hasn't let me down so far. And Damian may freak out a little when he finds out I'm a vampire. But if I stick to my plan and approach the subject carefully and break it to him gently, he might not run away screaming. Since he's into medical stuff, he might be interested and intrigued rather than scared. And I'll explain there's one big advantage of me being his girlfriend: he will never ever have to worry about me dying. That's something that should be *very* comforting to him.

CHAPTER 17

Florence | London, 1888

I tear off the ragged remains of my chemise and leap out of bed, feeling strangely energised. My arm doesn't hurt at all now. I unwrap the bandage and inspect it. There's nothing there! Not a cut nor a mark to be seen. The why or how of that is inconsequential. The only thing I have on my mind right now is Dr Dryden.

I crave him with an intensity that blocks out all rational thought except two: *I will find out what he's done to me, and then I will seduce him.*

It's not too difficult to discover his whereabouts. He's holed up in his study. I can smell him from the stairwell.

Ignoring the fact that I'm naked and my black hair is swirling in an unruly cloud around my shoulders, I bust through the locked study door easily and stand there like a feral Lady Godiva, sniffing the air.

Dr Dryden watches me warily from behind the desk. I sense he's afraid of me for some reason. No matter. I'm the one who's in control of this situation. Not him. I'm not sure what's happened to Florence Hughes, but I don't feel like a weak little governess anymore.

'Hello, my beauty,' he says as I take a cautious step forward, nosing for his delicious scent.

'What have you done to me?' I growl at him.

'What I had to.'

'You're not a doctor, are you?'

'I was once, a long time ago.'

I take another step forward. 'What happened? Did you kill someone?'

He smiles sadly. 'Something like that.'

I bounce on the balls of my feet restlessly. The urge to jump overtakes me. I sail through the air, landing with a thump on the desk, in the middle of his outspread newspaper.

Dr Dryden is taken by surprise, even more so when I launch at his neck, driven by an overpowering need to bite him. But I'm jerked back instantly—his fist twisting in my hair, holding me fast.

'Not so fast, my pretty temptress.'

'But I want ...' I whine.

'I know what you want. Rest assured you will get all the sustenance you need.'

I attempt to pull away, but it's fruitless; he has a tight grip on my hair, holding me from him like I'm a savage.

'If I let you go, Florence, will you promise to behave?'

I nod obediently. 'Yes, Master.' He slowly releases his hold on my hair. I crawl onto his lap and lie there curled into a ball, snuffling into his chest, while he gently strokes my back.

'Good girl,' he breathes. 'That's the way. Nice and gentle now.'

I can be his kitten, if that's what he wants. But I feel more like a bloodhound.

And there's something wrong with my mouth. My upper gums are aching unbearably. I rub at my lips, but it only serves to make it hurt more, and I whimper.

'Is your mouth sore? Let me have a look,' Dr Dryden says. He cups my chin, and I obediently tilt my head, allowing him to peel back my upper lip. He peers in and runs a finger gently along my gums, making me wince. 'Hmm, progressing nicely,' he mutters.

He bends towards me and licks my gums with his tongue right at the place where it aches the most. A moment later, there's a hot eruption. I moan in pain, fear, and rising horror as something sprouts in my mouth. *What is happening to me?*

'Hush now. It's all right. It's just your blood teeth coming through. I helped them along.' Dr Dryden cradles me in his arms, rocking me, but I feel anything but reassured.

'B-blood teeth!'

Gingerly, I open my mouth and touch each of my eye teeth. They feel like pointy fangs!

Something odd is also happening to my heart—it keeps racing in my chest and then faltering. It must be the shock, or I'm having a heart attack. *So this is how my life ends— sitting naked on a false doctor's lap in Belgravia, with bizarre teeth.*

Dr Dryden places his forearm on the desk and makes a small incision on his wrist with a knife. Blood droplets appear along the line of the fresh cut. He dips his finger into the blood and smears it on my gums.

'This will help ease the pain,' he says, and the relief is instant, like a soothing balm.

I don't know how or why it does as I'm too distracted by the taste of his blood and the delicious smell of it emanating from his wrist. It's too tantalising to ignore. He holds his wrist to my mouth. 'Feed a little. It will help with the transition.'

Instinctively, I place my lips on the cut and suck. The flow of Dr Dryden's blood gushing into my mouth is ambrosial. Tears leak from my eyes as my heart gallops and slows. Gallops and slows. Gallops ... and stops. I shudder and jerk against him, blood dripping from my lips onto my white thighs. *Oh, I'm dying. I'm dying!*

'Forgive me, my darling,' Dr Dryden gasps, clutching me to him. 'Forgive me.'

Why is he saying that? Why is he begging for my forgiveness? It's not his fault.

I reach up to touch his face (it's the last one I'll ever see) as I struggle to breathe, straining, gasping for air. Then an excruciating pain shoots through my entire body, and I slip down into a velvety black embrace. *Oh, merciful God, at least it's going to be quick.*

***

My tomb is in utter darkness. But somehow, I can feel with utmost precision the slippery cold silk sheets against my skin, every single spring of the mattress I'm lying on.

As my eyes adjust, the room slowly comes into focus and sharpens with unnatural clarity. Thick velvet curtains are tightly drawn, and the room is bathed in violet light, dust motes suspended like stars. I blink in wonder.

'Welcome back, my darling.' I turn my head towards *his* voice. Dr Dryden is sitting with his legs crossed in an armchair by an unlit fireplace, and I can see every pore on his translucent skin.

'What happened?' I ask, sniffing the air as a lovely scent

tickles my nostrils. Dr Dryden pushes up off the chair and walks over to me. The scent—*his* scent—intensifies, making my mouth water.

He kneels by the bed and takes my hand. His touch is a comfort in the midst of bewildering uncertainty.

'You died, my darling.'

Disbelief and horror roll through me as his words sink in. *I died? I'm dead?* 'W-what?' I whisper. 'But why are you here too? Are we in heaven?'

Dr Dryden's mouth twitches, as if he finds this last question funny. 'No, we're not in heaven, my dear. But you, me, Charlie—we are all dead or undead actually. Creatures of the night. Nosferatu. Or if you prefer a more popular term: vampires.'

'Vampires ...' I run my tongue over my teeth, feeling the sharp points with a shudder. 'I've heard the name, but I thought it was just folklore. W-what does it mean exactly?'

Dr Dryden squeezes my hand. 'It means we are immortal, Florence. We don't grow old, and we can't die, not from natural causes anyway. We can eat flesh. But to keep strong and healthy, we must drink the blood of the living—and from each other ...'

Revulsion and curiosity shoot through me, and Dr Dryden gives a low chuckle, as if gleaning my emotions.

'But it is a most pleasurable experience,' he adds. 'Will

you let me show you? I promise it won't be painful.'

I nod, trusting him. But why I trust a man who's turned me into a creature of the night, I don't know. Rising, Dr Dryden sits beside me on the bed and brushes back my hair from my breasts. He leans forward, and two sharp needles sink into my flesh. I gasp from the intensity, but he's right: I feel no pain, only a thin trickling pleasure that grows into rapture as he sucks from the wound, his hand reaching down to simultaneously stroke between my legs.

He's not going to stop this time. I won't let him, I think determinedly.

Dr Dryden huffs a soft laugh. He redirects his mouth to my nipples, and his tongue laps and toys while I moan and writhe beneath him. His fingers thrust inside me and I open my legs wide, shuddering with excitement in the violet light, which is now as bright as day.

'I am all yours, Master. *Take me*,' I moan.

Dr Dryden stands and swiftly sheds his jacket and waistcoat, then begins unbuttoning his trousers.

'Oh yes, my beautiful girl,' he says with a smile, his white fangs dripping with my blood. 'I plan to.'

CHAPTER 18

Damian | Edinburgh, present day

After Florence leaves, I bury my head in the pillows, cursing my stupidity. *Why the hell did I tell her about Juliana?* Now she's going to see me as the dude with the dead girlfriend. It will put her off, like it's put off the majority of my friends, who have slowly drifted away from me. My family was brilliant when it happened, but now even they're reluctant to mention her name in case it sets off my anxiety. Which is what's happening now.

I inhale deeply, exhale, and repeat it several times to slow my breathing, like my therapist taught me. My lips burn a little as I breathe. They feel slightly sensitive, like when you've brushed your teeth, step outside, and take a breath of freezing winter air. Is it Florence's doing? She *really* needs to get her circulation checked if her lips are that cold.

After five minutes or so, my breathing calms, and I start feeling a bit silly lying here in my underwear. *Should I get dressed? She's taking a while. Maybe they've run out of teabags, and she had to go out?*

I reach over the side of the bed, ease my phone out of my jeans pocket, and lie back on the bed, checking my messages.

There's one from my brother.

Bro! Florence is hot. You should definitely go there. (Don't tell Amber I said that!) Talk to you later. PS: Hope her leg is ok after the Cujo attack. (crying with laughter emoji)

I roll my eyes. Andrew is a pain in the arse at the best of times. But he's my only sibling, so I have to put up with him.

Not bothering to reply, I click off my phone, lean over, and slide it back into my pocket. As I do so, I happen to glance under the bed and see the edge of a book. Must be Florence's bedtime reading ...

Stretching my hand out as far as it will go, I grasp the edge and draw the object slowly towards me. I'm expecting a historical tome. But when it appears, it's not a book at all. It's thin, square, and has a gold clasp on the edge of it. The spine is ragged, and the whole thing looks really old. A family photo album? Or has she bought it off Etsy? Florence is so into the Victorian period that I wouldn't be surprised. My fingers brush over the faded black cover with flower and vine embossing, unsure if I should open it. But a photo album isn't a diary by any means. So I feel I'm quite within my rights to have a quick peek.

Unlatching the gold clasp, I carefully open the album to the first page. A sepia-toned Victorian portrait is mounted on the black card. A smile spreads across my face as I gaze at the image of a young dark-haired woman. Wow, it is a family photo album. Despite the old-fashioned dress and hairstyle and her serious expression, Florence's resemblance to her great-grandmother is uncanny.

I turn the page. Florence's great-granny is now dressed in a 1920s flapper dress complete with a jewelled feather headband. The black-and-white photo isn't formally posed. She's leaning against a wall, looking slightly away from the camera. The image is blurred, as if the photographer had a dirty lens. But it can't be the same woman if it's the 1920s, I reason—it must be her grandmother.

I turn to the next page, which has another black-and-white photo. The same fuzzy woman is now dressed in capri pants and has a 1960s beehive hairdo. She's sitting in an armchair, looking up and laughing, as if the photographer has said something funny. Her hand is raised as if she's about to cover her mouth but hasn't quite got there in time. *Is this now her mother?* I wonder, feeling bewildered. But she looks *exactly* like Florence. She even has the same slightly twisted left lateral incisor.

Heart pounding, I turn to the next page, but it's blank. Quickly, I flip through the rest of the album, but there are no further photos. I'm about to place it under the bed again. But something makes me lean over, take my phone out of my jeans pocket, and snap a quick shot of the 1960s photo—then another, zooming in on the woman's teeth. It's not uncommon for dental traits to be hereditary, but an exact match to a parent's teeth is rare. I probably shouldn't check her dental records just to satisfy my curiosity ... But it's bugging me. I'll just have a quick look tomorrow. I mean, this has to be her mother. It can't be Florence; she's only in her twenties. Even if she uses Botox, it's not *that* good.

A door bangs shut in the distance. I hurriedly shove the album back under the bed, scoot under the covers, and lie there innocently with my eyes closed, as if I'm napping.

'Hey,' Florence says softly. I crack open an eye to find her perching on the side of the bed. She offers me a mug of tea.

'Thanks,' I reply, sitting up to take it.

She smiles at me, and I can't help staring at her teeth. *The exact same teeth in the photo.* There has to be a rational explanation because the irrational one is mind-blowing.

'Everything all right?' she asks, noticing that my hand holding the mug is shaking.

'Yeah, just recovering from a slight panic attack. It happens if I talk about the accident. Sorry for getting all emotional.'

I take a gulp of tea, practically searing my lips.

Florence tucks a hot-water bottle with a pink knitted cover under the covers, and it rests warmly against my thigh. The heat from it is actually quite comforting. It's sweet of her to get it for me.

'Well, you don't have to apologise, honestly,' she says. 'It must have been awful for you.'

I take another sip of scalding tea so I don't have to answer. 'Are your flatmates home?' I ask to change the subject.

Florence nods. 'Yes, one of them. Sadie and her ... man.' She twists her hands in her lap, and her impeccable long purple nails catch my eye. I feel bad that she may have got them done especially for Sunday lunch. Not only has she been attacked by my mother's dog, but she's also been forced into playing emotional nursemaid to me. To repay her kindness, I've been nosing around in her personal stuff. What a creep!

I gulp the rest of my tea guiltily. 'I should probably go,' I say. 'But thanks so much for this.'

'Oh, are you sure? You can stay if you like. I'm not up to anything. We can chat or—'

I shake my head. 'I've got stuff to do at home. But I'll message you, if that's OK?'

'Sure,' she says, sounding disappointed, and takes the empty mug from me. I struggle into my jeans underneath the covers, not really wanting to put on a show in my boxers.

Florence hands me my trainers silently as I button my shirt, and I sit on the bed, jamming my feet into them without bothering to unpick the laces. My phone with the illicit photos is burning a hole in my back pocket. I can't meet her eyes. But as I go to pick up my coat from the armchair I laid it on, I notice she's not looking at me anyway. Her focus is trained on the side of the bed I've just vacated.

Chapter 19

Florence | Edinburgh, present day

Damian is ghosting me. I message him three times on Monday, and he leaves me on read. It's driving me up the wall—literally. When I'm sick of pacing around my bedroom, I climb up the far wall and huddle in the dark corner like a sad spider, willing him to message me back. But my phone stays silent. It's a monumental crisis. However, it's my own fault. I should have hidden that damn album well out of sight. Before he left, his mind was a whirlwind of confusion about the photos he'd seen in there.

On Tuesday, I cave under the pressure and call a flat meeting for that evening, knowing that Sadie is going to be mightily pissed at me for what I'm about to suggest.

We settle into our usual seats: Sadie in her revolving chair. Hester and I on the bare leather couch, which smells slightly of bleach. It's usually covered in a tartan blanket, but that's been removed because Sadie said it required heavy-duty dry-cleaning due to blood spillage. Apparently, she had to give the entire dry-cleaning business a memory wipe in case they called the police.

'What's this about, Floss?' She sounds tired, which isn't surprising as memory-wiping ten people would take it out of you.

'We have a mild crisis,' I say, deciding to downgrade the situation from 'monumental'.

'If it's about your dentist, you know my opinion—'

'He found my photo album,' I interrupt before she can say anything further.

Sadie's eyes narrow. 'Photo album? I thought we agreed not to have any photos since it was damning evidence of our immortality,' she says in a low voice.

Hester nods in agreement.

I gulp. Little do they know, I used to have a whole lot more photos, and I did burn some of them. But when it came down to it, I couldn't get rid of *all* of them. I wanted some proof of my existence. But I've broken a cardinal rule of our coven: when something has been decided by a majority vote, you have to adhere to it—and we agreed unanimously about the photos back in 1976.

'How many photos are there?' asks Sadie.

'Three. Late nineteenth century before I was turned. One from Paris in the 1920s. That was a pretty bad photo, by the way. And one from the 1960s at our McLaren Road flat. I thought keeping those three would be OK as it looked generational—you know, great-grandmother, grandmother, and mother. But Damian wasn't convinced. He spotted my teeth are the same in the 1960s photo and was curious. The last thought I picked up was that he wanted to check out my dental records. I don't know if he did or not as I'm out of range, but the fact that he ghosted all of my messages yesterday suggests he knows there's something fishy going on.'

Sadie stares at me. 'You read his mind?'

I lift my chin, feeling chuffed with my new power that only works with one person. 'Yes, I did.'

Hester claps. 'That's great, Floss!'

I grin. 'Thanks. Uh, for complete transparency, I may have had a small issue with biting him on our first date and him running away. But I managed to give him a partial memory wipe. He remembered having a date with me, but not coming here.'

Hester whistles. 'Go, Floss! At least you tried to fix it.'

But Sadie groans. 'You stupid idiot. If you'd come to one of us, we could've done it properly.'

My smile falters.

'Hey,' says Hester sharply. 'No name-calling. Floss fucked up, but it's easily fixed. I'll just memory-wipe him tonight, and she can change her dentist.'

'No!' I blurt out before I'm forced to take the safe route. 'I-I've decided that I want to tell him about who I am … about all of us. He's important to me. But you need to agree to that, hence why I called a flat meeting so we can vote on it. Mine's obviously "yes".'

Sadie's cobalt eyes darken, and her lips thin. 'My vote is "no". You don't tell him. I don't want a human knowing about us—even if he is *important* to you,' she says flatly.

I nod. No surprise there. 'Hester?'

Hester doesn't say anything and chews on her bottom lip. My stomach clenches in fear. If she says no, then that's it. It will be like Damian and I never met. I'll never get to talk to him or kiss that sweet mouth of his ever again. And I'll never know what it's like to be in a proper caring relationship and to have him know the real me without this godawful secret hanging over my head. I stare at Hester, pleading with puppy dog eyes. *Please please please.*

'My vote is "yes". Floss can tell him. But on one condition—that you offer him a choice: either be turned if he wants a relationship with you or a *complete* memory wipe if he doesn't.'

I balk at that. 'Neither of those is something I want to do.'

Hester shrugs. 'It's safer for him. If Alexander ever discovers our whereabouts, your dentist will be the first to die. Turning him will at least give him a fighting chance.'

I digest this in silence, knowing she's right but hating that she is. It's bad enough that I have to reveal my true self to Damian. But asking him if he wants to be turned? Fuck. Who would willingly choose that? Neither Hester, Sadie, nor I was given any choice in the matter. He's never going to agree to it.

'Look on the bright side,' says Hester, seeing my mournful face. 'If he does agree to be turned, you'll have a hot immortal boyfriend—and that's loads better than having a hot thrall boyfriend.'

Sadie makes a growling noise deep in her throat and vacates the room in a blink of an eye. Her annoyed voice permeates my head: *I'll be in my room cursing both of you if anyone wants me.*

'You didn't need to say that,' I tell Hester. She's looking amused, so she's obviously been given the message too.

'Oops,' she says, not sounding sorry in the slightest. 'The bleach she used on the couch must be addling my brain.'

I feel guilty for causing flatmate conflict. 'Why did you say "yes"?' I ask in a small voice.

'Sadie has Elliott ... in some capacity ... If Damian's your heart's desire, I think you should be allowed a chance at love. It's your life, Floss—and it's going to be a long, lonely one without someone special to share it.'

'Well, thank you ... I think,' I say. 'In a way, I wish I hadn't met him. At least I wouldn't be dealing with this.'

'Don't say that.' Hester doesn't quite meet my eyes, and I suddenly realise why she voted like she did.

'Oh no, not you too! What's his name?'

'Will Knight. He's in my drama class. He doesn't know I exist.'

'I don't believe that for a second.'

Hester is striking: tall, flaming auburn hair, green eyes.

'Let me rephrase that. He *acts* like I don't exist. And since he's pretty talented, he's good at making me believe it.' She huffs a laugh.

'What do you know about him?'

'Honestly, nothing much. I just ... listen and lurk—and drool from afar. It's pathetic, really.'

'Oh, Hester ...' If anyone deserves to be happy out of the three of us, it's her. She's spent 500 years looking for the right man.

'The weird thing is there's something familiar about him. I feel like I've met him before. But from where, I have no idea. It's really annoying.'

I grin. 'Well, I'm sure you've run into a lot of people since the sixteenth century, so it's not surprising he resembles one of them. Why don't you read his mind and find out more about him?'

Hester shakes her head. 'I tried that. Normally, I'd respect his privacy. However, I did get desperate once and tried to see if he had a girlfriend or a boyfriend. But I didn't find out much, except that he was looking forward to having KFC for dinner.'

Sadness flickers across her face; then she collects herself.

'Anyway, enough about me. More importantly, how are you going to tell Damian?'

'I hadn't thought about it. I was sure you were going to vote "no".'

My stomach flips. This is it. I'm going to tell Damian I'm a vampire—a guy that I'm starting to develop serious feelings for. If he chooses the memory wipe, it's going to crush me for years. I may never recover. My resolve wavers. *Don't be a coward, Floss.*

'Maybe invite him out for a drink and say you have something important to discuss?' prompts Hester.

'Yeah, a public place is best, I suppose.'

Hester nods. 'You don't want to make him feel like he's in physical danger and that he can't leave if he wants to. He might panic.'

I gulp and try not to imagine the worst: Damian skedaddling out of the bar as fast as his lovely muscular legs will carry him.

Chapter 20

Florence | London, 1888

On the fifth night, the three of us go out for supper. Dr. Dryden asks me to call him Alexander in front of Charlie, but to address him as Master when we're alone, since Charlie might grow jealous if he hears me referring to him like that. Ever since he turned me, Alexander has been trying to placate him. Apparently, I was meant for Charlie, to provide him with sustenance and sex. But Alexander took me for himself.

'Charlie is a man-child with no control over his appetite, Florence. His other governesses barely lasted a month, and he promises he'll try harder each time it happens. But there was something special about you—something strong between us. When he couldn't stop drinking from you, I didn't want you to die like the others, so I intervened. Once you drank my blood, you became mine, my darling.'

The 'man-child' is now throwing me frosty looks in the carriage as we head out of Belgravia. I was slightly nervous about being in such close confinement, but Alexander reassured me before we left, 'There is no need to fear, Florence. You are with me, and I will stop him this time if he tries anything. Besides, I believe you can hold your own now.'

One advantage of being a new vampire is that my strength is currently at its peak and why even Alexander was afraid of me at first. But he's my love, and I'd never hurt him. I don't even feel angry at him for turning me into a vampire as it is the only way that we can truly be together.

'Where are we?' I ask after we've been rolling over the cobblestones for at least half an hour. I twitch aside the black velvet curtain. Amidst the shadows and dim gas lamps are row upon row of run-down brick tenements. It's a far cry from the white icing elegance of Belgravia.

I'm under no illusion about what 'going out for supper' means since Alexander explained it to me in no uncertain terms. I'm just grateful he let me feed from him before we left the house, so I'm not involved. I'm simply there to observe the way things are done. The carriage driver is one of Alexander's thralls, always on hand to do his bidding. I haven't yet fully grasped how such human attachments work; all I know is that his thralls are carefully chosen and paid well for their services.

'On the outskirts of Whitechapel,' Alexander answers gruffly. 'It's not our usual playground. We usually go farther in. But there's a killer on the loose, which is making it difficult for us to feed. People are afraid and keeping indoors, and I don't want to arouse suspicion.'

'And it would be highly insulting if we're mistakenly arrested for the works of *that* amateur,' Charlie adds with a derisive snort.

'Have they not caught him yet?' I ask curiously. Of course I've heard about the murders—Spitalfields is near Whitechapel—but I haven't been paying much attention to the papers. My focus has been on feeding from my master, and making love with him as often as possible.

'Not yet,' replies Alexander, taking my hand protectively in his. 'But he tends to work later on in the evening and in the dark alleyways. We'll stick to the lit streets, where there will be more ... opportunities.'

Charlie gurgles in anticipation and rubs at his mouth. He hasn't fed since the incident in the dining room, and Alexander has been busy with me and not taken him out, so I assume his appetite is keen. He's not allowed to go out alone without Alexander's supervision. I suspect if he did, then Whitechapel police would have more than four murders on their hands to deal with.

The carriage judders to a halt.

'Now what happens?' I ask, and Charlie rolls his eyes, as if my constant questions annoy him.

'Now we wait.' Alexander holds a finger to his lips. 'Patience and quiet are key.'

We sit in tense silence while the horse shifts its hooves restlessly on the cobblestones.

Soon, there's a tentative tap on the window.

Charlie shifts slightly, and his head cocks. He nods at Alexander, who draws back the curtain. The friendly freckled face of a young woman appears at the window. She's wearing a blue dress trimmed with lace that's coming away from the neckline in places and a matching satin hat with bedraggled feathers.

Alexander lowers the window.

'Good evening. What can I do for you?' His tone is smooth and mellow, and the woman's eyebrows lift as she takes in his slicked-back hair, sharp cheekbones, and black evening suit.

'More like what *I* can do for *you,* mister,' she drawls, trailing a hand over her ample bosom.

Charlie leans forward then, revealing himself, and the woman's lips part as she rakes her eyes over him.

'Blimey,' she says. She drags her attention away from Charlie and focuses back on Alexander, her eyes now bright.

'If it's a duo, it's gonna cost yer more—twelve pence.'

'Just my son, but I'm happy to pay your price,' says

Alexander with a furtive glance at me, whom she hasn't yet seen.

The woman pouts but quickly agrees. He opens the carriage door and helps her in. Then he knocks twice on the ceiling, and the carriage takes off with a jerk, causing the woman to flop down next to Charlie in a flurry of skirts. My nostrils flare at the sharp scent of her cheap perfume.

She clocks me sitting there in my green dress, and her mouth drops open.

'Who are you? His mama?'

'Something like that,' I say stiffly. 'Good evening.'

The woman shakes her head as Charlie snuffles at her neck, and she whispers to him, 'Why are your mama and papa here? That's so odd!'

Charlie nods at Alexander, and he drops the curtain back, plunging the carriage into darkness—for the woman. The three of us can see perfectly well with our violet night vision.

'There you go. They'll just sit there in the dark, so you don't need to mind them,' Charlie purrs hypnotically. 'I'm the only one you need to worry about.'

The woman's eyes glaze over, and she doesn't protest as Charlie unbuttons the top of her dress and runs a hand over her breasts. She sighs and juts her hips as he toys with her nipples. Alexander's hand clutches my thigh, but his focus is trained on Charlie's 'lovemaking'. The woman's head lolls back against the seat, exposing her surprisingly elegant neck. Charlie laps at the column of her throat with long, slow strokes, and she emits a soft moan. Her skin looks none too clean, but he doesn't seem to care. He's taking his time even though I know he's desperate to feed. Is he putting on a show for me? So I can see what I missed out on?

Charlie moves his head to the woman's chest.

Despite knowing what's about to happen and having had it done to me on a nightly basis, it's still not an easy thing to witness. I turn my head away, but Alexander whispers, 'Watch how he does it. It's an art. You'll need to do the same soon, my dearest one. You can't keep feeding from me.'

I nod and force myself to watch as Charlie, fangs bared, sinks the tips into the skin directly above the woman's heart, delicately puncturing it.

Drops of liquid appear, then more. Charlie laps eagerly at the deep violet stream as it flows down between the woman's breasts. He makes an ecstatic noise in the back of his throat as it hits his system.

My eyes are fixated on the glowing purple blood, and I lick my lips. My blood teeth itch and burn as they extend, and I want to push Charlie out of the way and take my fill too. But Alexander's arm is vicelike around my waist, holding me in place. 'Easy, darling,' he whispers in my ear.

The woman moans, and I shift uncomfortably as Charlie makes another puncture. But he's too busy slaking his thirst to notice the woman's eyes have snapped open. She can't see the bloody mess on her chest in the darkness, but there's no doubt she can feel the sting of Charlie's fangs and his lapping tongue. She starts screaming at the top of her lungs.

Charlie quickly slaps a hand over her mouth. 'Shut the fuck up!' he growls. For some reason, his mind control doesn't seem to be working.

Alexander tuts. 'Do you want me to—'

'No, Papa. I've got it—oooof!'

The woman has kicked him hard in the groin and is now scrabbling for the door handle. Charlie yanks her back, and she screams piercingly. I look at Alexander, and his jaw is tight. I can tell he wants to intervene because all this noise isn't helping us stay discreet.

'Control her. *Now*!' he hisses.

'*Arrrrrgggh*!' the woman cries in terror as Charlie looms over her. She can't see his fangs but senses she's in mortal danger, which she is. Her eyes swivel wildly and search for me in the darkness. 'Ma'am, please! Help me, for the love of God!'

The heel of my hand presses against my nose, trying to

block the scent of her blood, which is driving me insane.

'Please, ma'am!' She's crying now, begging me to help her, and something twists in my gut. She is me, and I cannot let him do this.

I launch at Charlie, knocking him sideways against the carriage wall, gripping his lethal snapping jaw. He struggles to free himself, but I'm too powerful.

'Go. Quickly!' I tell the woman.

'Oh oh oh, thank you!' she gasps tearfully and lunges towards the carriage door.

I can't see what's happening behind me as I need all my strength to hold on to Charlie. *Let her go*, I plead with Alexander in my mind. There's a burst of fresh air (which, thankfully, whisks away the smell of blood from the carriage), then the sound of boots landing on cobblestones and scurrying footsteps. She's gone. She's safe. I sigh in relief.

But it's short-lived as Charlie wrenches himself out of my grasp and shoves me away from him. I hit the opposite wall at a weird angle, and my spine pops in protest. But I sit up and flex it back into position calmly. I'm not injured in the slightest. I don't need Alexander's protection after all. I'm too strong. Charlie can't hurt me.

'What the fuck did you do that for, wench?' he snarls, crouching in the corner. 'Now I'm going to bed hungry!'

'Florence did the right thing, Charlie,' interjects Alexander. 'Killing her was too risky, especially here.'

'I disagree, *Papa*. Rein your bitch in, or I'll do it for you.'

'Watch your mouth, *son*,' replies Alexander tightly. 'I won't have you speak about my wife like that.'

I stare at him amazed. *Wife?* Did we get married without my knowledge?

Charlie's lip curls disdainfully, showing a fang. 'How romantic. I'm so happy for the both of you.' He cracks his knuckles and glares at me.

The carriage has been meandering along aimlessly, and I have no idea where we are. We could be outside Buckingham Palace for all I know. But from the unsavoury smells curling through the swinging carriage door, I sense we've come farther into Whitechapel. The thought makes me uneasy, and I turn my head away for the briefest moment.

Charlie silently springs towards me, aiming for my neck, but Alexander is ready for him. I'm pulled out of the way and thrown unceremoniously from the carriage before he can do any damage. My cheek scrapes hard against grimy, wet cobblestones and I sprawl like an ungainly doll, my dress tangling round my legs. Spitting out bits of gravel and cursing Charlie, I leap to my feet, fists clenched, ready to deal with him myself.

But the carriage door has swung shut.

Alexander sticks his head out, looking grim. 'Sorry about that, my darling. Charlie is a little unsettled. So it might be best if you make your own way back, just for your own safety. Everything will be in order by the time you return.'

I gape at him. 'But ...'

'You'll be perfectly fine, my love. There's nothing out here that can hurt you.'

Charlie gives a low evil chuckle from behind his shoulder. 'If you happen to see Jack the Ripper, say hello from me, bitch.'

'No, wait! Don't leave me—' But before I can finish, Alexander knocks twice sharply on the carriage roof, and it swiftly drives off, leaving me alone in the heart of Whitechapel.

Chapter 21

Damian | Edinburgh, present day

After leaving Florence's flat late Sunday afternoon, I trudge back to my own silent, empty one. There's nothing to do but heat up a bowl of minestrone soup in the microwave for dinner and stand there watching it going round and round like the question in my mind.

Why does Florence so strongly resemble those three women in the photos?

The answer when it comes to me is simple, and I sag against the counter in relief. Because it *is* Florence, you dummy. Duh! Didn't she say her flatmate Hester was involved in the theatre? The actors must have held a few themed parties over the years, and she's dressed up and gone along too. The photos are just for fun. Admittedly, the faded Victorian one is extremely realistic ... But I push any doubt to the back of my mind. It's easy enough to recreate that old-fashioned look with the right props, and Photoshop has sepia-type filters.

The microwave dings. I slip on an oven mitt, feeling a lot

better that I've figured it out, and it's nothing weird at all. The savoury smell of the soup, when I extract it from the microwave, makes my stomach grumble loudly. It's been hours since lunch; maybe I'll have some cheese on toast too.

I'm lying on the couch after my makeshift dinner, absorbed in a sci-fi series and attempting to relax, when my phone dings. Probably Andrew trying to rile me again. I ignore it. Then it dings again ten minutes later. For God's sake, is he deliberately trying to piss me off? I pause the show and look at my phone.

It's not Andrew. They're messages from Dad.

Hi Damian, just checking in. I hope Florence wasn't too traumatised? Is her leg ok? Your mother is chatting to one of her friends on her phone in the lounge so I've come into the study for some DTO. Love Dad.

I chuckle at that. DTO means 'Dad Time Out', a polite way of saying Mum's animated conversation is getting on his nerves and he's over it. I move on to his second message.

Hi again, I've been racking my brains all day trying to remember where I'd seen Florence before. I was just having a flip through some of my old photo albums.

Check out the attached.

I open the attachment, and my heart skips a beat. Dad has taken a screenshot of a Kodak colour photo that features a group of youths at a party in a random lounge. From the clothes and the hair, it must be the 1980s. I recognise my lanky beardless dad in an AC/DC T-shirt. Standing next to him is his suave older brother, Tim, in a white linen suit à la Don Johnson. Tim has his arm around a pretty blonde girl with big teased hair. She's wearing a short leather skirt with a studded belt and a black halter top with a skull and crossbones. Her lips are scarlet red, and she's pouting at the camera. But it's the beautiful slim goth girl in ripped jeans and black leather jacket next to her that my gaze is drawn to. Her dark hair is short and spiky. But the purple lipstick, pale skin, and those violet eyes are unmistakable.

The photo is from a party at Tim's flat in 1983 (there was a date on the back). The quality isn't great, it must have been a bad batch of film, or someone didn't know how to use a flash, but the likeness of the dark haired girl to Florence is uncanny, don't you think? Her blonde friend went out with Tim for a couple of months. I can check with him but I'm pretty sure her name was Sadie ...

An icy chill runs down my spine as I gaze at the photo of the two girls. *Sadie*. Surely, this can't be ... Florence and her flatmate?

I remember Tim being quite upset at the time as they broke up suddenly. I think he must've really liked her. Anyway, maybe you can make better sense of it all than me. Love Dad.

I smile wryly at his closing sentence. Thanks, Dad, for opening Pandora's box, shutting the lid, then quietly slinking off. But his discovery is timely, and I can't ignore it. Based on this new evidence, Florence is not just an enthusiastic attendee of themed parties. She was actually *at* a party in 1983, *which makes her as old as my father*!

Bitsy going crazy at her for no reason.

Feeling no pain after being bitten.

Weirdly cold hands.

Her ageless appearance ...

Yeah, my freak-o-meter is back on high alert.

***

During my lunch break the next day at work, I check

Florence's X-rays against the 1960s photo I have on my phone. I'm 99.9 per cent sure that it's definitely her—not that it helps me much as, unlike Dad, I didn't think to see if there was a date on the back of the photo to prove it. But just thinking about the possibility that she's even older than my dad, like another twenty years older, blows my mind too much to even contemplate it. My emotions are all over the place.

Then I get a message from her, which makes me feel guilty on top of it. Like she somehow knows I'm sitting here, poring over her dental records while eating my tuna salad sandwich. Her message is nothing pointed, just friendly.

Hey how's it going?

But I can't bring myself to reply in a similar tone as if nothing's wrong. So I leave it and concentrate on my afternoon patients.

On the way home after work, I receive another one. Still friendly, but slightly more worried.

Hey Damian, did you get my last message? Hope your day went well.

I leave that one too.

By the time I reach my flat, my anxiety is building momentum, about to take off like a speeding car without a driver. My hand is trembling so much it takes a couple of tries to slot the key into the lock. Once inside, I slam the door and lean against it, dragging in deep lungfuls of air. I laugh at myself a little when I've calmed down. I'm acting like she's stalking me, for God's sake.

Pull yourself together, Dr Rhodes.

It sounds like something Florence would say.

I have every intention of replying to her after I've had a long relaxing hot bath, but then I decide to cook myself a healthy dinner and listen to a podcast.

So I don't.

I'm zoned out on the couch, listlessly flicking around Netflix, unable to settle on any particular show, but wanting something—anything—to keep my mind off her when I receive another message.

Hey, is everything all right? If you're sick let me know and I'll come round and take care of you. I owe you one after Bitsy (winking emoji)

The subtle implication that she'll do more than serve me chicken soup causes goose pimples to scud along my arms and my cock to harden spontaneously. I'm too scaroused to know how to reply.

So I don't say anything.

***

That night, I toss and turn, unable to fall asleep. My therapist would probably say the extreme anxiety I'm experiencing is a natural reaction after what happened with Juliana. I'm having feelings for someone. Therefore, I'm protecting myself so I don't get hurt again.

But it's more than that.

There's something in particular about Florence that 10 per cent of my brain understands perfectly and the other 90 per cent is desperately trying to flee from.

Around 2 a.m., I drift off and start having a vivid dream. I'm hovering in a purple light above Florence's bed. She's down below, curled up in white silk sheets. Upset. Crying because I haven't replied to her messages. 'I'm up here!' I call, but she keeps on sobbing. I flail my limbs around, but I can't force my body to go lower. There's some trick to it, but I can't figure out what. It's so frustrating.

Then I look down, and the bed is empty. Where did she go?

There's a tap on my shoulder, and I slowly roll over to find her hovering above me so we're face to face. I reach out for her, drowning in her intense violet eyes. Her lips don't move, but I hear her say distinctly, 'Don't leave me, Damian. I need you.'

I wake with a start to find my arms sticking up in the air like I've been holding onto someone. Lowering them, I sit up and flick on the bedside light. It's freezing cold in the room, but I'm overheating, my thin T-shirt clinging to my sweat-covered chest.

Blindly, I reach for my phone, determined to message Florence right now despite it being 3 a.m. But when I unlock my phone, I see she's sent me another message *five minutes ago*.

Damian, there are some things I need to share with you. Can you meet me at The Brief Encounter on Friday at 7pm? If you don't show then I won't bother you again. You have my word.

I reply with: *OK, I'll be there.*

Switching off the light, I snuggle down under the duvet, exhaling quietly. Florence isn't denying there's something weird going on, and I'm finally going to hear the truth. Part of me is reluctant to hear what that truth is, but there may still be some rational explanation. At least that's what I'm telling myself.

Chapter 22

Florence | Edinburgh, present day

In all my long years of being a vampire, I've never revealed it willingly to anyone before or given them the choice of being one themselves. So understandably, I'm a little nervous about meeting Damian.

There's not a lot I can do to prepare for it either. Hester suggested I take the subtle approach rather than going in all guns blazing. So I'm going to drop vague hints and let him work it out for himself. Hopefully, he doesn't freak out too much. But I'm bracing myself for the inevitable.

I fly over to Stockbridge well before 7 p.m. in case there's an event taking place in the football field like last time, but it's all clear. So I end up sitting in the bar alone, nursing a glass of water, waiting for Damian to arrive. When it flicks past 7 p.m. and he hasn't shown up yet, I wonder if he's changed his mind.

But he said he would be here.

Then he is, standing in front of me with a half smile. My lip quivers as I return it.

'Hey,' I say weakly.

He rakes a hand through his hair nervously and glances at the bar. 'I'm going to grab a whisky. Do you want a Bloody Mary?'

I shake my head. 'No, I'm good, but thanks.'

He strolls off, and I let my gaze linger on his retreating form. Drinking in the way he walks, the tilt of his head as he leans against the bar, the way his two-toned hair falls over his cheekbone as he speaks to the barman. His long fingers digging in his back pocket for his wallet. This could be the last time I see him, so I want to memorise every little detail ...

'Slainte,' says Damian, clinking his glass against mine when he's seated with his drink. He takes a gulp of whisky. Up close, he has dark circles under his eyes and looks like he's had a few rough nights. I know the feeling. I don't need seven hours of shut-eye, but I've been struggling on the two hours I normally have.

'Slainte,' I reply and swirl my water.

'So', he says, 'there's some stuff you want to tell me?'

His tone is neutral, but his shoulders are tense. I don't need to read his mind to know he's still weirded out about those photos.

I nod. 'Yes, before we ... I mean, if you want to keep hanging out with me, you should know that ... I've had a bit of an odd life.'

Damian's eyes meet mine steadily. 'What do you mean by "odd life"?'

I shift in my seat. 'Uh, I've had to move around a lot. And when I lived in London, there was some ... drama.'

'Drama? You mean with an ex?' he prompts. I can tell he's really just wanting me to tell him outright, but it's better for his mental health if I don't.

I lean back against the padded banquette and steel myself to keep going. 'Yes. My ex-boyfriend ... he's looking for me. And there'll be ... consequences ... if he finds me.' *Namely having my neck snapped.*

Damian frowns. 'Is he Russian?'

I stare at him blankly. 'Ah, no. At least I don't think so? But I'm not entirely sure of his background...'

'Right. I think I get what you're implying.'

My shoulders sag in relief. *Thank goodness.* He doesn't even seem too upset about it. Perhaps I was worrying about nothing.

Damian leans in closer and says in a hushed voice, 'I can see why you can't say it outright. They may be listening.'

His eyes swivel right, then left like one of those comedy spyhole paintings.

'Who exactly?' I whisper to make sure we're both on the same page.

'*The mafia*,' he whispers back. 'Your ex-boyfriend is heavily involved, and you're in a witness protection programme.'

He leans back in his chair and takes a sip of whisky, looking pleased with himself.

What? Oh no!

He's so far off the mark it's not funny.

I sigh inwardly. 'That's not it, Damian,' I say, trying not to let my frustration show. 'I'm not on the run from the mafia.'

'Oh.' His face loses the smug expression. 'Well, what then? Just tell me. It can't be that bad.'

I open my mouth, then close it again.

'Perhaps I will have a Bloody Mary.'

'Fine.'

He goes off to the bar, and I attempt to collect my thoughts. The subtle approach isn't working. I'm going to have to give him a massive hint, maybe something I couldn't possibly know unless I was there at the time.

'Here you go.' Damian puts the drink down in front of me.

I take a sip and try not to wince at the taste. Anything other than blood tends to resemble vinegar.

He's got himself another whisky too.

'So where were we?'

'London, 1888,' I blurt out suddenly. 'You've heard of Jack the Ripper, I take it?'

Damian nods. 'Of course. It's one of the most famous murder cases in history. What's that got to do with anything?'

'He was my height. His breath smelled like fish. He was right-handed. The blade was going to draw from left to right—here.' My eyes are closed, my palm perpendicular against my neck.

'It was almost intimate, the way he whispered in my ear, telling me to keep still and it wouldn't hurt a bit.'

I open my eyes to find Damian staring at me, white-faced. 'What the fuck, Florence? Are you having a past-life experience?'

'No, I was there. I was nearly one of his victims.'

Damian's eyes almost bug out of his head. He takes a sip of whisky, then another larger one and returns the glass to the table with a shaking hand.

'I'm not crazy, Damian, and I'm not into woo-woo mumbo jumbo.'

He jerks as I feed back to him what he's just been thinking. 'How did you do that?'

I shrug. 'Mind reading is one of my powers. But only with you, it seems, and only within a certain range.'

'P-powers?' His face drains of colour further, and he

fumbles with his phone. He brings up a photo, and I twitch. Here we go, he's going to confront me with hard evidence. But it's not the photo I think it is.

He brandishes it in front of my face.

'Is this you? And your flatmate?'

I take his phone and look at the photo with nostalgia washing over me. *Wow, I'd forgotten I had short hair in the 1980s. I was really into Siouxsie and the Banshees back then. Sadie looks badass too. That was when she was with Tim. But how the hell does he ... ?*

I look closer at the teenager on the other side of Tim and see the resemblance to Damian immediately. I let out a surprised laugh. 'Oh fuck! Seriously? Is this your dad? That's so wild. He has got a good memory for faces.' *Shit, what are the chances? Now I'm going to have to memory-wipe his dad!*

Damian groans and places his head in his hands and shakes it violently. 'This isn't happening. This isn't happening.'

'Damian—'

I reach out to touch his hand, and he jerks away from me. 'It might be easier to deal with if you have another whisky. It's my round anyway,' I say stiffly.

I leave him at the table and go up to the bar, trying not to feel upset by his reaction. It's not surprising under the circumstances, but still ...

Maybe I shouldn't have led with the Jack the Ripper story, it's a bit extreme. But it's also one of my defining moments, and I'm quite proud of the way I handled myself.

CHAPTER 23

Florence | London, 1888

What was Alexander thinking leaving me in Whitechapel, alone, with no money and a killer on the loose? Trying not to think about that, I start walking quickly in a westerly direction—or what I think is west since I have no idea where the bloody hell I am. If this is an initiation test, I don't think much of it.

At least I can see in the dark, and I'm glad I'm wearing sturdy boots if the need to run presents itself.

The stinking street is devoid of people at this late hour, and a thin misty fog hangs in the air. There's no sound, but the tap of my muffled footsteps on the cobblestones and the faint rumble of chatter from a drinking establishment a few streets over. My original family live in Whitechapel somewhere, but I haven't seen them since Aunt Ivy plucked me from an even worse poverty at 8 years old. They washed their hands of me and left us to it. How would my parents and siblings react if I turned up on their doorstep now, as a vampire?

I'm amusing myself with thoughts of how that would go when a lone carriage appears, horse hooves clopping loudly on the cobblestones. It slows as it reaches me, and I turn away in annoyance, cursing Alexander for leaving me here like a harlot. The carriage resumes its steady pace when I don't approach it.

I unclench my fists and take off at a faster trot in the opposite direction.

I'm passing by a stretch of wooden fencing when something seizes me around the waist, and I'm pulled through a narrow opening. It happens so quickly I don't have time to react. My face is squashed roughly against the fence and my wrists wrenched behind my back. When I start to scream, a meaty hand slides over my lips and I bite hard into a fleshy finger. The owner gives a yelp. 'Bitch!' a male voice growls in my ear. Before I can punch his lights out, I'm yanked backwards by the hair and dragged across a courtyard with a hand clamped across my mouth. None of this hurts, but it is making me incredibly angry.

'You're a lively one, aren't you?' His rasping kipper breath is so rank it makes me gag.

He hauls my body over into the far corner, away from the street. I go limp, letting him think I've fainted from shock. It suits my purposes: I'm going to rip his throat out, and the fewer people who hear it, the better. My blood teeth are aching with anticipation. I'm a far more dangerous killer than he is, and he's about to become my first victim. *Good riddance.*

He releases his hand from my mouth, and crouches beside me. I bare my fangs but tense as a slim sharp blade presses against my throat. 'Keep still, and this won't hurt a bit.' His stinky fish breath wafts over my face, and my nostrils flare at the indignity. The stench of kippers will *not* be my last memory.

'You chose the wrong woman, *Jack*!' I hiss.

Twisting my head and ignoring the sting of the knife's blade as it skims my throat, I champ down on his arm. The woollen material of his coat is no protection for my lethal teeth. I rip out a large chunk of flesh, spitting a mess of gore and fibres onto the cobblestones. His blood coats my lips and dribbles down my chin.

The knife clatters to the ground as he sinks to his knees, moaning in pain. I give a low chuckle of satisfaction and scramble up a brick wall, discovering that I can cling to it without any effort. Clambering to the top, I crouch there, licking my lips. Below, Jack clutches his arm and scrabbles for the knife. He brandishes it wildly, peering into the darkness.

'Up here, *jackass*!'

He sucks in a breath, seeing me outlined against the night

sky.

'I'm going to gut you, you little bitch!' he growls.

I arch an eyebrow. How rude. It's about time I taught this man some manners.

I spring from the wall, aiming directly for his throat.

He doesn't know what hit him.

***

I arrive back at the house, blood spattered and ready to tear a strip off Alexander—literally. Growling to myself, I stomp up the stairs with my fangs out. *He's going to pay for dumping me in that hellhole.* Yes, I managed. But that isn't the point. He's supposed to *care* about me.

I find him in his bedroom, standing at the window, facing the door as if he's been waiting for my return. A copper tub of steaming water sits between us. He holds out a finger and beckons me forward.

'Come, my darling. Let's get you cleaned up.'

I snarl and ready myself to pounce.

'I know you're angry, my dear. And yes, I deserve it. And you can say anything you like to me. But first, let me wash you and look after you.'

His velvety smooth voice wraps around me, and my resistance dissolves. I wilt like a fading flower, powerless beneath his will. A hot bath does sound good, and Alexander looking after me sounds even better ...

Tilting my head back, Alexander gently rinses my soapy hair with clean, warm water from a flowered jug. The bathwater turns a pretty shade of pink.

'Where's Charlie?' I ask.

'Sedated. I fed him some of my blood mixed with a special serum I've been working on for vampire insomnia. It seemed to do the trick.'

I don't say anything. Not for the first time, I wonder what else he's been dabbling in down in his basement laboratory, which I'm forbidden to enter.

Finished with my hair, Alexander scoops it to one side over my shoulder, soaps a washcloth, and begins making slow circles over my back. I purr in contentment.

'I was thinking', he says idly, 'that three vampires under the same roof isn't necessarily the best arrangement.'

Instinctively, my body tenses, wondering what he means by that. *Am I going to get thrown out on the street?*

He chuckles, reading my thoughts as he's apt to do. 'I would never, my precious one. I simply meant that we should take a trip.'

My taut muscles ease slightly as he rinses the soap off my back. 'A trip? Where to?'

'How would you like to go to Paris?'

I swivel in the bath and look up at him. 'Paris! For how long?'

Alexander cups my cheek and smiles indulgently. 'Just for a couple of months, my love. To give Charlie some space. I'd hate for anything to happen to you.'

Anger bubbles up in me. 'Humph, you didn't seem too worried when you dumped me on Jack the Ripper's doorstep!'

Alexander strokes my cheek soothingly with his thumb. 'Shush now, my darling. I had complete confidence in you, and you handled the situation beautifully.'

'Yes. Well, Jack won't be bothering anyone else from now on!' I growl, and Alexander's lips quirk.

'That's my girl. But Charlie is more dangerous than a common street killer. I thought he would be mature enough to handle our relationship. It seems he isn't.'

'Can't you just keep sedating him?'

Alexander purses his lips, as if considering it. 'That's a possibility, but it's not a long-term solution. I'd much rather get you away from him completely, let him feel the consequences of his jealousy.'

I shrug, not really caring about Charlie and his emotional problems. He's brought it on himself. Besides, I'm excited by the thought of a trip to Paris with Alexander. 'Yes, all right. If you think that's best, Master.'

'I do, indeed …' He leans forward and kisses me deeply. I close my eyes, returning it, relishing his attention. *And I want you all to myself*, he says huskily in my mind. His icy hands reach into the cooling water to cup my breasts, and I shiver in pleasure.

Let us go to bed, my queen. I wish to make love with you and share blood before the sun comes up, in celebration of your first conquest.

I nod eagerly, and Alexander takes my hand. Under his adoring gaze, I emerge like Venus from the bath, rosy-tinted water sluicing off me. I feel like the most powerful woman on earth. I feel like a god.

Chapter 24

Damian | Edinburgh, present day

Tilting the bottle of Jack Daniel's to my lips, I slug it straight back and slump against the pillow. Adding more alcohol on top of the two whiskies I had at the bar isn't smart. But after the night I've had, drunken oblivion is preferable. I just want to slip underneath the duvet and get some respite from my thoughts. But how I'm supposed to deal with the woman I like being a vampire, I'm not sure. I groan out loud and take another large gulp.

Outside, the wind is howling and rain is lashing down, which only adds to my misery. Even the weather agrees. It's the perfect night for an all-night binge drinking session.

I must doze off for a minute or two (or fall unconscious) as I'm woken by the smell of alcohol and a burning sensation on my chest.

Shit. I quickly right the dribbling whisky bottle, which has created a large wet patch on my T-shirt. Capping it and placing the bottle on the floor beside the bed, I drag a weary hand across my face and pluck at my T-shirt. But I can't be bothered getting a fresh one. Nothing's changed.

It's still raining.

I'm still alone.

And Florence is still a vampire.

I close my eyes, feeling slightly nauseous from all the whisky I've drunk. But despite that, the moment she admitted it to me is imprinted on my mind. We sat there, looking at each other after she came back from the bar and handed me a whisky. I took a steadying breath. My brain was telling me not to ask. But I had to know.

'So w-what you're trying to tell me is t-that you're a *v-vampire*?' I stuttered, my mouth as dry as a bone.

'Shh.' She glanced quickly over her shoulder. 'Keep your voice down. This is privileged information. But yes, I am.'

All I could manage was a choked gurgling sound in reply. Then—and this is the bit that I'm not particularly proud of—I acted like a frigging cold robot, thanking her politely for whisky and chucking it back in one. The worst thing was that she didn't seem surprised at all. Just sat there, looking at me sadly as I grabbed my coat and legged it out of there.

Determined to erase her beautiful face from my mind forever, I reach over the side of the bed for the bottle. But before my fingers touch it, I become aware of a steady tapping on the window.

What *is* that? Hail? A loose aerial?

Stumbling from the bed, I swipe back the curtains and freeze in terror. It's her. Florence. Hovering outside my window. Dressed all in black, dark hair whipping like snakes around her pale face. She taps on the pane and indicates that I should let her in. I whip the curtains shut, stumble back to the bed, and collapse on it.

Holy fuck, how drunk am I? Now I'm hallucinating about her!

The tapping begins again.

After five minutes, by which time I've convinced myself I'm having some kind of alcoholic-induced nightmare, I lever myself up off the bed and shuffle over to the window. I peek through the curtains, and my gut trembles. She's still there. My eyes slip to the pavement below. Oh my god, I'm in a top-floor apartment and four storeys up. Yet she's *levitating* ...

There's a sharp rap on the window to get my attention.

Reluctantly, I slide my eyes back up to her.

'Damian!' she calls out. 'Please let me in. My hair.' She points to her long locks, which are admittedly getting severely tangled in the wind, and pulls a mournful face.

I chuckle a bit at that, albeit with a tinge of hysteria. Florence wants me to let her in because her hair is getting messy.

She grins when she sees me smile and presses her palms together in a praying motion. 'Pretty please,' she mouths.

Fuck it, I think. *What's the worst that can happen?*

Duh, being eaten alive by a vampire woman—that's what! says my common sense, which is desperately trying to claw its way to the surface of the whisky lake of my mind. *But surely, if she wanted to kill me, she would have done so by now?* I reason. I'll take my chances.

A gust of wind and rain hits me in the face as I heave up the sash window as far as it will go.

Florence sinks down to ledge level and hovers there. *What is she waiting for?*

'You have to invite me in,' she says.

'Oh.' So that rule does actually exist. 'Florence Hughes, please come into my room,' I intone solemnly. *And please don't eat me*, I add silently.

Stepping aside from the window, I gape as she slithers through and lands lightly on my bedroom floor. I inch backwards, my heart thumping in my chest. *Shit, I've done it now.*

Florence closes the window and looks at the puddle of water she's making on the floorboards, then at me. 'Sorry, I'm dripping,' she says.

'Don't move. I'll get you a towel.'

In the bathroom, I catch sight of myself in the mirror.

My cheeks are flushed, and my eyes are unusually bright—I actually look pleased that I'm entertaining a vampire. I give myself a stinging slap. *Snap out of it, you fool!*

My cheek smarting, I drag a clean towel from the cupboard and scurry back to my room.

'Here you go.'

'Thanks.' Florence takes the towel and winds it around her shoulders, dabbing at her face. Her black leggings and long-sleeved black T-shirt are sopping. It's the first time I've ever seen her wear modern clothing.

I don't suppose she'll catch her death, but it's polite to ask.

'Do you want a change of clothes?'

'Yeah, that would be great. Thanks.'

Busily, I fetch a clean pair of grey joggers and a plain white T-shirt. I consider adding a pair of boxers too, but that would be weird.

'Bathroom's through there. Have a hot shower if you like,' I hear myself saying. 'Or a cold one, if that's what you prefer. I don't know how it works ...' I throw up my hands helplessly.

'It's either or depending on my mood,' she says, giving me a quick smile. 'But thanks. I might, just to freshen up.'

I hop back into bed, switch on my bedside light, and listen to the water running and the sound of humming.

There's a naked vampire in my shower, I think wondrously. It feels surreal.

When Florence comes back in, she's wearing my clothes, her hair is slicked back (she's used my comb!), and she's towelling it dry. She sits at my desk and swivels in the chair. I'm transfixed, unable to tear my eyes off her. But she seems unconcerned at the attention and checks out the titles in my bookcase. She indicates my copy of *Interview with the Vampire*.

'Nice,' she says, looking over at me with a grin.

I smile weakly and wedge myself deeper into my pillow. *Dammit, I don't even have a crucifix ...*

'How did you find out where I live?' I ask.

She shrugs. 'That sort of thing isn't difficult for me. I was out anyway, doing some scouting, thanks to Sadie. She's paranoid about Alexander ... my ex-boyfriend ... showing up. So after that, I decided to check in on you, to make sure you were OK ... after our chat.' She eyes the half-full bottle of whisky on the floor. 'Sorry for interrupting your tête-à-tête with Jack Daniel's.'

'What does scouting involve?' I ask to get her off the subject of my drinking. I reach down and hastily shove the bottle under my bed.

'Climbing to the top of Scott Monument,' Florence says.

'Right.' I nod but inwardly balk. *Climbing Scott*

Monument? What the fuck? That is not a normal activity for someone to be doing on a Friday night!

She finishes towelling her hair, pulls a knee up to her chest, and plays with one of my pens, looking at me.

For some reason, watching the smooth cylinder slip backwards and forwards between her fingers is quite arousing. She sees me watching and smiles flirtatiously.

'So how are you doing, Dr Rhodes?'

I take a breath and will my cock to behave. 'Absolutely fine.'

'Really?'

I nod. 'Uh, admittedly, I was a little *surprised* to find out that you're undead. But apart from the initial shock, I think I'm handling it pretty well.' My words slur a little, and Florence huffs a laugh.

'So you'd be fine if I came and joined you over there on the bed?'

I gulp, knowing the right thing to do is exclaim loudly, 'Stay back, creature of the night!' and hold up my fingers in a cross.

But instead, I chirp brightly, 'Sure!'

I close my eyes in despair. *What the fuck are you doing, you idiot?*

When I open them again, she's right there, crouching on the end of my bed. Looking at me with an expression of wary vulnerability. Like a puppy expecting me to kick her. I can't help it; it melts me.

'Come here,' I say, holding out my arms. In a flash, she's there, her body pressing against mine, her face inches away. She rubs her impossibly smooth porcelain cheek against mine while I stroke her back.

That dried-roses scent winds around us, and I breathe it in, understanding now that it's not her perfume—it's vampire pheromones: compelling, alluring, dangerous.

With a smile, she lowers her lips to mine, and the sensation is like tasting an ice cube. But it's not unpleasant; it's actually quite refreshing, chasing away the grogginess of the whisky. As the kiss deepens and Florence gently rubs her hips against my crotch, I can feel my cock hardening and my resolve to keep my distance slipping. Then it hits me.

Oh my god, I'm being seduced by a vampire. I'm so royally screwed!

CHAPTER 25

Florence | Edinburgh, present day

Damian is hyperventilating, which is concerning as I thought we were making progress. I levitate over his body so I'm not touching him, but that seems to make it worse. His eyes practically bug out of his head.

'Sorry, I know this is a bit weird—'

'A bit weird?' he chokes out. 'It's fucking *insane*.'

I grin. 'You haven't seen me climb the walls and hang out on the ceiling yet ...'

His breathing intensifies. Not to mention his heart rate is going double time and pumping all that juicy blood around his body. It's making me feel hungry, and my fangs start aching. *No, Floss, do not even think about it!*

Staring into Damian's dilated pupils, something breaks inside me. This is not the face of a man who is considering having a relationship with me. He's currently focused on staying alive.

I need to give him more reassurance.

'Damian ...' I swallow nervously since this is the first

time I've admitted my feelings for a man in over a century. 'I like you. A lot. I ... I want you.' My voice tremors, and suddenly, I can't look at him—I feel too vulnerable.

'To ... eat?' he asks warily. My eyes flick back to his and note that he's pressing harder into his pillow to create more distance between us.

I huff out a laugh. 'No. Well, not unless you want me to.'

A flash of desire or possibly unbridled terror passes across his face.

I touch his chest briefly, and he flinches. 'I'm joking, Damian. You have my word I won't take blood from you without your permission. Now or ever.'

I mentally cross my fingers, hoping he doesn't ask if I've taken any from him previously. *I didn't mean to. It was just a little taste.*

Damian's eyes search my face, and I feel like I'm standing on a knife-edge. 'Please believe me. I really do like you. I can't stop thinking about you. You're haunting my dreams.' I stroke his cheek, and his facial muscles lose their tautness, and he begins to breathe more evenly. I smooth his hair back from his forehead, and his eyes hood slightly at the touch of my fingertips.

'You really like me?' he asks at last. 'And you won't hurt me?'

'I really, *really* like you, and I *definitely* won't hurt you.'

He breathes slowly and evenly as I gently trace his eyebrows and twine my fingers in his hair. At least he's allowing me to touch him rather than screaming. That's a good sign.

'OK, I know I shouldn't probably believe you, but I do,' he says at last and rolls his eyes heavenward. 'God help me.'

I almost tell him that God won't help him, just as he never helped me. But I don't want to ruin our fragile equilibrium.

Lowering down onto his chest, I kiss him softly, tentatively. Then when he doesn't pull away, I kiss him harder. Our tongues meet, and we explore each other curiously. It's an affirmation that tells me his mind as well as his body are opening up to me, and there's a glimmer of trust there. And it's kind of hot. I suck gently on his tongue to deepen the trust (or perhaps slake my lust), and Damian moans softly against my mouth, his arms slipping around me. One of his hands lowers to the small of my back, and I can't help grinding experimentally against his hard length to let him know I'm not against the idea of—

He breaks our kiss with a gasp.

'Can I ... can I just ask you something?'

'Uh, sure.' I drag my focus reluctantly away from his cock. 'Yes, ask away.'

'How exactly do you ... feed?'

I slide off him into the space next to the wall and prop my head on my elbow, resting my cold bare feet against his warm ones.

'We have a trusted source,' I explain. 'Sadie's ... friend ... Elliott. He runs a blood donation centre from his flat. It's mainly uni students looking for some extra cash. He drops blood bags off at our flat on a regular basis.'

Damian frowns. 'So he gives you untested blood? Blood that could have all sorts of diseases? I'm not sure I approve of that.'

I shake my head, feeling a twinge of pleasure that he cares about me—to a small extent anyway. 'We're impervious to disease. Besides, Sadie is very strict about him only using students with a clean bill of health from their doctors ...' I trail off, not wanting to go into too much detail.

But Damian, being interested in the physiological aspect, is now pressing a thumb into my wrist, trying fruitlessly to locate a pulse. His hand lifts to my neck, and he pauses. 'Can I?'

I nod.

He presses three fingers into my throat, then moves them again, then again. 'Oh my god,' he murmurs incredulously after a few seconds. 'This is seriously fucking with my head. I have so many questions.'

'And I don't want to keep anything from you.' *I'll tell you what I think you can handle.* 'I'm putting it all on the line here.'

'Are you?'

'Yes! I've never told anyone I'm a vampire.'

Damian nods seriously. 'I can see why, Florence,' he says, slipping into his sexy professional dentist voice, which makes me want to laugh.

'Please call me Floss,' I beg. 'It makes me feel like I'm back in the nineteenth century when you call me Florence.'

'Floss,' says Damian slowly, like he's trying it on for size. He doesn't say anything, then lets out a chortle.

'What?'

'A dentist with a girlfriend called Floss. I mean ... It's kind of hilarious.'

I frown and stare at him. *Girlfriend?* I intone in his mind.

'I mean ... I thought ... only if you want ...' he says, blushing and back-pedalling madly.

Pure happiness floods the mausoleum of my soul. *Definitely*, I purr with a smile. *I thought you'd never ask.*

***

I can hardly believe it. Damian is fine with me being a vampire, and I'm now his girlfriend! And I didn't even encourage him to ask me. This is going a lot better than I expected. I still have to tell him about the choice he has to make: either be turned into a vampire or have a complete memory wipe. But I'm hopeful if he likes me enough to date me, he'll choose being turned. Fingers crossed.

'I'm going to get a drink of water. Do you want anything?' Damian looks at me enquiringly, and I shake my head. 'Actually, do you drink tea or coffee or anything? I've never seen you.'

'No. I can, but it doesn't taste so great.'

'But you had a Bloody Mary at the bar?'

I pull a face. 'I prefer the real thing.'

He nods. 'Ah, right. Not sure Uber Eats actually delivers blood bags, but I can check.'

I laugh at that, and he throws me a grin. Once he's gone to the kitchen, I shift underneath the duvet and wiggle contentedly in the warm indentation he's left, covering myself in his scent. Mmm, I'm definitely feeling in the mood for some action now. I remove the clothing he lent me and pull up the duvet to mostly cover my breasts. I'm assuming a lot here—that Damian will let me stay over and that he wants to have sex with me. But since he's now *my boyfriend*, I'm hoping he's up for it—on both counts.

Damian stands stock-still in the doorway when he returns. His eyes rake over my bare shoulders.

'You look comfortable in there,' he says.

I twirl an end of my hair provocatively around my finger. 'I am. Would you like to join me?'

He sucks in a breath and walks over to the bedside light and abruptly switches it off. *I'll take that as a yes.* He quickly lifts off his T-shirt and slides down his boxers.

Does he think I can't see him because it's dark?

'You know I have night vision, right?'

'Oh shit.' He claps both hands over his privates, and I snigger to myself. It's a bit late for that!

He takes a step forward, and there's a dull thud.

Damian gasps in pain, holding one hand over his cock while the other clutches at his foot.

'Oh no, poor you! Come here.' He hops over to the bed and practically collapses on top of me. Luckily, I can bear his weight easily. Diving down to the end of the bed, I gingerly check each toe in turn while he groans.

'Which one actually hurts?' I ask.

'The big one, on the left. I don't think it's broken. But fuck, it hurts.'

'I'll give it a rub.'

There's silence while I rub his toe and give it a little kiss for good luck. Damian's breathing quickens.

Either he likes his toe being kissed, or he's worried I'm going to bite it off.

My hand travels from his foot, trails up his shin, and reaches his solid, shapely thigh.

'Anything else need rubbing?' I run my hand lightly over his cock, and hear him swallow.

'That definitely does.'

'I don't want to take advantage of you when you're drunk.'

'Funnily enough, I feel completely sober now. Which is probably a good thing if you're about to have sex with a vampire,' he quips.

I keep stroking his slowly stiffening cock, 'Oh, so we're having sex, are we?'

Damian groans. 'Not if you keep doing that, we won't be. It'll be all over rover.'

I reluctantly remove my hand. 'So no more foreplay then?'

'Well, maybe not for me. But you, on the other hand ...'

Damian snakes an arm around my waist and hauls me down next to him. He covers my breasts in kisses, sucking at my nipples; electricity zings straight to my pussy. Ooh, I like feisty Damian.

'God, you're perfect,' he murmurs, brushing a hand down my body. 'How did I get so lucky?'

I huff a laugh. 'Most men wouldn't consider a naked vampire in their bed "lucky".'

'Apparently, I'm not most men.'

He draws small circles on my stomach, and I tense in anticipation. But he's taking his time, trailing a hand over my thighs, and exploring me in his thorough doctorly way. Finally, a finger slides between my legs and I let out a small moan as it glides over a highly sensitive spot.

'You're so wet,' he whispers, sounding surprised. 'I thought it would be dry down there.'

'It's venom,' I reply, my eyes closing in pleasure as he plays with my clit and rubs around my entrance. 'Vampires don't have normal bodily fluids like humans.'

'Venom. Intriguing. So if I licked you, would I get affected by it?'

My thighs quiver as he teases my clit some more.

'This is probably not the best time to have a physiological discussion,' I say, jaw clenching as I squirm under his touch. 'But yes, you'd get a buzz of energy.'

'But not turn into a vampire?'

'No, I'd have to bite you for that.'

'Oh. Where?'

My eyes lock onto Damian's neck, where a vein visibly pulses beneath his skin, and his blood—warm and honey sweet—is just out of reach. I trace the spot lovingly with my tongue, fangs aching in anticipation in case he's going to let me feed a little.

Damian squeezes my clit, and I jerk back from his throat, letting out a gasp of pleasure.

'So you'd like that, would you? To feed off me while we have sex?'

Oops, I may have accidentally projected that thought into his mind.

I nod vigorously, mouth watering. 'Oh, yes please.'

He chuckles, brushing his lips against mine. 'You can have the sex, but not the biting.' His tongue touches the tip of a fang as if testing it for sharpness. Then draws away.

I pout. 'Tease.'

'Or just self-protective. I'm not sure I'm ready to be sucked on mid-orgasm. But never say never.'

'We can work up to it,' I say huskily. 'Soooo just sex for now...'

'Yes, for now ...'

He glides his cock along my slick folds, slowly and deliberately and I shiver, arching my back, wanting all of him. 'I'm assuming I don't need a condom?'

Oh god, this is really happening. 'No, no condom required.' I reach down and guide him to my entrance, catching his heated gaze as I do.

'Let me know if I hurt you,' he whispers. 'I'm not small.'

I smirk. 'You'd need an elephant cock to hurt me. Just saying.'

He huffs a laugh. 'Good to know.'

In one smooth, deep motion he thrusts inside and I gasp feeling the stretch but he fills me perfectly. Damian grunts against my neck. 'Fuck Floss, you feel so good taking my cock,' he says in a throaty voice.

My eyes widen, and I almost combust from that alone. 'Are you talking dirty to me, Dr Rhodes?' I growl.

He laughs. 'Yeah, do you like it?' But then gasps as I scrape my nails down his back.

'God yes, it's as sexy as hell. But don't ever use that voice on your female patients. They'll come in your chair.'

He chuckles and lightly traces his tongue over my lips, then kisses me. 'It's all for you, pretty girl.'

I shudder as desire sparks along my spine and I wrap my legs around his waist, rolling my hips eagerly to match every stroke. Damian's terror must've taken a back seat to his lust as he's thrusting and kissing me with abandon, and whispering filthy things in my ear, not caring about my extended fangs that nip dangerously close to his neck. Right, if he likes it risky—

I flip him over as if he were a Ken doll and lift us into the air. His surprised 'whoa' turns into a groan as I slide down onto him, but he lets me take control. His complete trust, despite the fact he's being ridden by moi in mid-air, is impressive and kind of comforting.

My body hums with pleasure and power as I ride him, grinding down again and again.

Damian's hands clutch at my hips as he moans incoherently. 'Oh god. Don't stop, too good. I'm gonna come—'

'Me too,' I gasp, and my back arches as I climax; a sharp crescendo that sends my senses spinning. Then another waves crashes, dragging us fast and furious into the undertow. We groan simultaneously in pleasure.

When I eventually look down, Damian's gazing at me in post-orgasmic bliss, chest still heaving, starry-eyed.

'That was ... frigging magical.'

'Pretty amazing,' I agree. I lean in for a kiss, my body sated with him, my thoughts heavy with bloodlust—but I forget we're still in mid-air.

We collapse onto the bed in an ungainly heap. The frame gives an ominous crack, then tilts sideways and dumps us against the wall.

'I think I need to order a new bed,' Damian says after a shocked pause.

I huff a laugh, brushing hair out of my eyes. 'Yeah, one that can withstand vampire bonking.'

CHAPTER 26

Florence | Paris, 1888

I'm trying on a new dress, admiring my muted reflection in the bedroom mirror, when Alexander drops a newspaper onto the dressing table. 'I thought you might be interested in this.'

The headline screams 'Jack l'Éventreur Frappe à Nouveau!'

Curiously, I pick up the newspaper and scan it. But even after a month in Paris, my French is still hideously poor since I'm not mingling with humans to practise. 'Bonjour', 'au revoir', and 'je veux sucer ton sang' are the extent of my language skills. Alexander, of course, is fluent. That's why he suggested coming here. He can parley-voo with anyone.

'What does the headline say?' I demand.

'It says, "Jack the Ripper Strikes Again". Apparently, there's been a fifth female victim. I can tell you the details if you want, but this one was extremely gory and distasteful, so I don't advise asking me.'

Alexander removes his shoes and lies on the bed, closing

his eyes. His face wears a sated expression. It's the look he gets whenever he's been out prowling the streets of Paris for supper. He never tells me where he goes or what he does. He says it's best I feed from him for now and don't ask questions.

I stare at him. 'But that's impossible. There must be some mistake. I drained that bastard and ripped him to shreds.'

Alexander shrugs, still with his eyes closed. 'It's probably someone copying him because they want the fame. I wouldn't rattle my crypt over it if I were you.'

I leap onto the wooden chest at the end of the bed and crouch there, growling.

One of Alexander's eyes cracks open, and he sighs.

'Are you miffed, my love?'

Miffed is the understatement of the century. 'We have to go back to London. *Now*,' I say in a low dangerous voice to impart how important it is.

'Back?' Alexander echoes. 'What on earth for?'

'So I can find the second killer and finish him, of course!'

Alexander tuts. 'Just let the police do their job. It's none of our business.'

'But I can *help*, Alexander!' I cry in frustration. 'The police aren't doing anything. They don't even realise it's someone else!'

Alexander licks at the corner of his mouth with his

tongue, then looks at me carefully. 'Don't go getting a god complex, Florence. You're not some kind of saviour. We keep in the shadows. We keep our heads down.'

'What if it's Charlie?' I hiss. 'Would that change your mind?'

Alexander reaches across for a manicure stick to clean dried blood from underneath his fingernails. 'I can tell you right now that it's not Charlie. He may be impulsive, but he's not stupid enough to leave a mess like that. Now drop it please.' There's something definitive and slightly threatening about that last sentence that makes me decide not to push my luck.

Chastened by my master, I jump off the chest and head over to my usual spot by the window. Being a vampire in Paris isn't as fun as I thought it would be. Alexander refuses to take me out with him in case I can't control myself. So after I wake up at dusk, I prowl around our townhouse, waiting for him to return. Most nights, I stand by the window, looking out at the rooftops and at the people strolling past in the street below.

But this evening, he did bring me a new dress after I complained that wearing dead women's clothing was creeping me out. That shows he listens to me some of the time—even if he is actively ignoring all my other grumbles about being left alone.

'I was thinking I should write to Aunt Ivy,' I say, turning around from the window. 'What if she visits your house in Belgravia and I'm not there?' *And Charlie lures her inside and takes a bite out of her neck to spite me.*

'She won't,' says Alexander, lazily scratching his own neck. 'I wrote to her when we first arrived and said that we were in Paris on a short family holiday. And, as my son needed to keep up with his lessons, I had invited you along too. So I've saved you the trouble.'

He undoes a cufflink and rolls up his sleeve. 'Come, my little governess. It's time for your supper.'

I slink to the bed, hating that I can't control myself when his blood is on offer. It tastes like sweet honey pouring down my throat and tingling through my veins. It's the highlight of my existence. And when he makes love to me and takes his own fill, our nightly ritual is complete. My master washes me clean of all the anger and discontent I hoard. He shows me my true purpose: I'm here to serve him.

***

I'm bored. Bored bored bored!

Alexander has just gone out *again* and left me to my own devices, but within the confines of the house. I'm starting to wonder if I'm really such a risk to society or if he's embarrassed to be seen with me. Or is it something else?

I stand at the window in my nightgown, watching him leap jauntily into a carriage below in his evening black. *He's just keeping us both fed*, I tell myself. But after six months of this, it's getting harder to believe Alexander's motivations are purely altruistic.

Opening the Juliet balcony doors, I step outside and lean on the railing, enjoying the feel of the cool night breeze on my skin. With my excellent vision, I can see Parisians in the opposite apartments, enjoying their evenings. There's a couple eating supper together, a woman reading a story to her child in bed, a woman playing the piano for a small group of people. My old friends—anger, despair, and loneliness—well up in me, and I close my eyes and clutch the railing tightly. This is what Alexander has taken from me. I might have got married, had a child, or at least had friends. But no. I'm stuck here alone in Paris for the foreseeable future because Alexander doesn't seem to have any intention of going back to London.

I let out a 'feeling sorry for myself' whine. I can't even cry because vampires apparently don't do that.

Glancing along the rooftops, I get a glimmer of an idea— a way that I can escape this prison.

But I can't do it in a white nightgown.

Setting my jaw determinedly, I head back inside and

proceed to fashion myself a climbing outfit from Alexander's one-piece black woollen long johns that he never wears. They're too big for me, but I roll up the sleeves and cut the feet off. I pull on some black socks and my boots, then tuck my hair under a black knitted cap I discover in his drawer.

When I'm done, I stare at my wavering reflection in the mirror and let out a giggle. I look ridiculous, like a beggar who's lost his jacket and trousers. But unless anyone decides to take a nightly stroll along the rooftops, my appalling fashion sense is safe from prying eyes.

Back out on the balcony, I nimbly scale the drainpipe, all the while watching the houses across the street in case anyone happens to look out. But the squares of yellow light are now plunged into darkness. It's past midnight, after all, and only the creatures of the night are out and about.

Reaching the top of the guttering, I clamber over the eaves and crawl up the roof valley, careful not to disturb any tiles. The slate is slippery, but I make it to the top without any trouble. Standing upright on the ridge of the roof, I'm delighted to find I now have an excellent view of the city. I can see right across Paris.

Somewhere down there, Alexander is biting someone's neck. The thought makes me laugh, even though it's not particularly funny. My daring escape, and the relief of being outside, is making me giddy. But if Alexander's going to be all mysterious, why can't I have a few secrets of my own?

I dance a little jig in the moonlight, congratulating myself on my cunning and—

My foot slips.

One second, I'm enjoying myself; the next, I'm rolling down the other side of the ridge. Before I careen over the edge of the eaves, I manage to hook my fingers over the guttering and hang there precariously with my legs dangling over the back garden.

I let out a nervous chuckle. That was close! It's a sizeable drop into the garden below, at least six storeys, and I'm not sure what would happen if I let go. Would I bounce or break my legs? I have no clue, having never been in this position before.

Fortunately, I don't have to find out because I can simply swing myself—

The old lead guttering gives a jolt under my weight as I move my hips, and a part of it tears away from the wall. Instantly, I keep still, my fingers digging into the metal to adjust my grip. I hiss out a curse.

The guttering gives another jolt. I let out a tiny scream as the part I'm holding on to pulls out of the wall entirely, and I'm suspended in mid-air.

I squeeze my eyes shut, waiting for the sickening drop

and the thud ... But nothing happens. There's no rush of air or crack of breaking bones. Slowly, I open my eyes to find myself hovering, still clutching the ancient piece of guttering. I fling it into the bushes below, and my body bumps lightly against the side of the wall.

I make a breaststroke motion with my hands but go nowhere. I kick my feet, but that's ineffective as well. *How the hell do I get back onto the roof so I can go inside?*

But that's the trick. As soon as I focus on the rooftop and kind of *will* myself, my body moves of its own accord, and I rise and land lightly on the ridge.

A thrill rushes through me.

Oh my god, no wonder Alexander is hell-bent on keeping me locked up inside.

I can fly!

CHAPTER 27

Damian | Edinburgh, present day

The main door of the Ramsay Garden flat gleams blood-red in the moonlight, and a trickle of fear runs down my spine. Accepting that Floss is a vampire and that she means me no harm is one thing, but meeting her vampire flatmates is quite another. It seemed like a good idea the other night when we were discussing it in my broken bed. Now I'm not sure at all. But she's my girlfriend, I care about her, and I want to be a part of her world—so that means meeting Sadie and Hester.

'They don't bite,' says Floss in a teasing tone, and I give her a withering look.

'This is not the time for those kinds of jokes,' I say snippily, my voice breaking.

'Sorry,' she says, squeezing my arm. 'Look, I know you must be scared. If you're not up to it, we can do it another time.'

I square my shoulders, not wanting to look like a lily-livered fool in front of her. *For God's sake, Rhodes, are you a man or a mouse?*

But my knees are trembling, and at this moment, I would have to say I'm very much a scared little mouse.

'Have they ... you know?' I make a vague gesture around my throat area, not quite sure how to put it or wanting to give offense.

Floss smirks. 'Had dinner?'

A cold sweat breaks out across my shoulder blades. 'Uh, yes. That.'

She checks the time on her phone. 'Elliott was due an hour ago, so I'd say they would have. And they know that you're coming over, so they wouldn't want to make you nervous by sniffing at you or anything.'

I smile at her weakly. 'Right.'

'We don't have to stay for long. It's not like you have to hear their life stories or anything. Jesus.' She rolls her eyes. 'You'd be here for *days* ...'

I can't help chuckling at that, which eases my tension. Floss's sense of humour is very dry. It's one of the reasons why I like her so much. I slide my hand into hers.

'You'll be right there too. You won't leave me alone?' I hate the way my voice quavers, but I can't help it.

She squeezes my hand so tightly my knuckles crack. I wince, and she eases off the pressure. 'Of course I won't leave you alone,' she says soothingly. 'I'll be right next to you the entire time … Though if they do decide to go for you, I'm not sure how much help I'll be.'

My eyes widen in terror, and Floss grins at me. 'Sorry, couldn't help myself.'

As soon as we step foot into the entranceway and Floss closes the door behind us, I know there's no going back. I force down my fear and trail behind her as we walk down the hallway, which has dark-blue patterned wallpaper.

'Huh, they put the lights on for you. That's nice.' She gestures at the half-a-dozen candle-shaped lights mounted to each side of the wall in sconces. 'Even Elliott doesn't get that kind of welcome.'

Knowing that Elliott Blythe—Sadie's friend or boyfriend or whoever he is—is here and fully aware of this coven is a relief. He and I are in the same position. Even though I know nothing about his relationship with Sadie, I'm hoping we can be friends. Allies.

The hallway leads into a sizeable lounge and double bay windows that face out over the city. A large leather couch faces away from me. Two people sit on it, close together as if talking, their backs turned to us as we enter.

'Here we are!' announces Floss overly brightly, grasping my arm possessively. 'Damian, meet my flatmates, Sadie and Hester.'

Two women rise to their feet, and I can't help gawking. From all the books I've read and movies I've seen, I know that vampires are supposed to be uncommonly beautiful; it's part of their power to lure you in. Floss is certainly stunning, and now I see that her flatmates—a slightly shorter blonde with a chin-length bob and a taller redhead with a long plait—are gorgeous too. Both have piercing stares that make the contents of my stomach liquefy. But as terrifying as they are, my fear is replaced by reverential emotion at being in their presence.

A compelling urge to kneel before them washes over me. I start sinking down to do so, and Floss yanks me back up.

'Stop that, for God's sake!' she says to the blonde, sounding annoyed. 'Don't kneel, Damian. She's just trying it on with you.'

The compulsion fades, and the blonde girl's scarlet lips twist in a smirk. I recognise her from my dad's photo. *Sadie.* She looks exactly the same as she did in 1983, apart from the sleeker shorter hair, and she's wearing different clothes; a black crop top and a green sequined skirt. Her belly button sparkles with an emerald jewel. I smile back warily and say 'Hello', pleased that my voice doesn't wobble.

'And this is Hester.'

The redhead is dressed more demurely in black wool trousers and a grey batwing top, as if she doesn't want to be noticed. But she's so tall it's difficult not to. She steps forward with a pleasant smile, and I instinctively put out a trembling hand. 'Hi, Hester. Nice to meet you.'

Hester is around my height, six foot, with wide slanted green eyes like a cat's, pale skin, and sharp cheekbones. She hesitates looking at my hand, then glances at Floss, who nods. She slides her glacial palm into mine and gives it a couple of pumps.

Nice to meet you too, Damian Rhodes. I've heard a lot about you.

Her voice sounds loudly and clearly in my head. When Floss does it, it always sounds soft and muted, kind of like whispering. But this is like tuning in to a high-frequency radio. I jerk my hand back in shock.

'Hester, leave him alone!' says Floss immediately.

Hester gives me a cheeky grin. 'Sorry about that. Nice to meet you, Damian.' She sits back on the couch, crossing her long legs.

Floss rolls her eyes at me. She seems on tenterhooks, as if she's worrying what her flatmates will do to me next. It's kind of funny, yet terrifying.

'And this is Elliott.' Sadie's voice is low and husky like she's smoked two packets of cigarettes and a cigar.

She moves aside, and I see that there's a third person. A guy in his late twenties is lying on the couch. He's dressed eclectically in a tweed jacket, blue-and-white striped collared polo shirt, and olive-green trousers. One brown suede booted foot taps to the music he's listening to via neon-blue over-ear headphones. He seems to be in his own little world.

She nudges his arm. 'Elliott, we have company.'

He opens his eyes, sits up, and removes his headphones, which emit the tinny sound of Wham!'s 'Club Tropicana'. With his blond hair flopping over his forehead and blue eyes, he looks remarkably like a young Cary Elwes. He even has the same 1980s haircut as him. But his cheeks are rounder, and the tortoiseshell-rimmed glasses he's wearing give him an intellectual look.

His eyes crinkle when he clocks me.

'Welcome to the madhouse, mate.'

I like him instantly.

CHAPTER 28

Florence | Edinburgh, present day

I think the whole 'meet the flatmates' thing is going well, even after the initial pranks by Sadie and Hester, which I was not amused by. Damian's pulse has slowed considerably at least. I'm grateful to Elliott for sitting him down on the couch and asking polite, but interested questions about what's involved in getting dental implants, which is a subject dear to Damian's heart.

Hester trails after me when I head to the kitchen to make Damian a normal coffee and Elliott a 'revitalising' one. She gazes longingly at the blood bag after I pour a little into Elliott's coffee.

'We could have "cocktails"?' she suggests.

But I feel shy about imbibing blood in front of Damian. 'Maybe another night.'

When we come back, Damian and Elliott are nattering away happily like a couple of old women. But I note that Elliott is being careful not to give anything away about his past and keeping the discussion firmly grounded in the present. I know he's doing it because he doesn't want to scare Damian. So it's going to be up to me to explain that Elliott's a thrall if he starts asking questions. Oh joy.

Then to my horror, Sadie—obviously wanting attention—drops a conversation bomb. 'Have you told Damian about you-know-what yet, Floss? He has to decide soon,' she says brightly and digs her elbow into my ribs.

Damian throws me a curious glance, and I stiffen as Sadie smirks, knowing damn well I haven't. A muscle twitches in my jaw, and I'm a hair's breadth away from biting her. *No, Sadie, I have not told Damian that he needs to choose between having his memory wiped or being turned into a vampire! So shut the fuck up!* I yell at her silently. The corners of her mouth tilt upward, but it's not funny.

This is a conversation that needs to be approached delicately because if I muck it up, the results could be catastrophic—namely I'd lose Damian forever. The thought is too distressing to even contemplate.

Hester gives me a sympathetic look and soothing one-to-one telepathy: *She's just jealous, Floss. Don't let her rile you. You'll handle it just fine.* One advantage about Hester having even more powerful mind control than Sadie is that she can cut her out of our mental dialogue anytime she wants to. It drives Sadie nuts.

And she knows she's doing it too because Hester's eyebrows are fluttering slightly. Sadie gives us an evil glare, and I can sense she's about to blurt something Damian's not ready to hear. So I say to him abruptly, 'Hey, do you want to come downstairs for a bit?'

Damian blushes bright red, and Elliott sniggers. 'Aren't you supposed to be showing him your etchings in the attic?'

'Yes. Well, an evil witch has commandeered the attic,' I say stonily, throwing Sadie a 'don't mess with me' look.

I feel bad about dragging Damian away from Elliott when they were getting on so well, but I can't risk Sadie deciding to take matters into her own hands.

However, as soon as we reach my lair and I shut the door, Damian faces me and folds his arms. 'What did Sadie mean? What haven't you told me?'

Oh, damn her to hell.

'It's nothing,' I say hastily, avoiding his eyes and walking over to the fireplace.

'Floss, whatever it is, please just tell me. Because the fact that you're not is truly frightening.' Damian's voice cracks, and I know I'm causing him unnecessary angst.

Maybe I should choose the memory wipe for him ...

I sigh and sit down, gesturing to the other armchair. 'Take a seat, and I'll explain. But you're not going to like it.'

Wordlessly, Damian sits across from me and waits.

I gather my thoughts. Perhaps if I explain how this came about, he'll understand better.

'Soooo you know how I told you that my ex-boyfriend is looking for me?'

Damian nods.

'His name is Dr Alexander Dryden, and he's the man who sired me. My human life ended in London on the night of 3 October 1888.'

Damian blinks once and doesn't say anything. So I take that as a sign I should continue. 'I ... I did something ... bad ... to him. Sadie was involved too. Thanks to Hester, we've been hiding out in Edinburgh ever since so he can't track us down.'

'Why thanks to Hester?'

'As she's way older than us, Hester's powers are more advanced. She's able to shield me from Alexander's blood bond, also known as a "sire bond",' I explain to him. 'It acts like a homing beacon, allowing him to find me if he's within a certain range,' I add when Damian looks blank. 'We recently found out that Alexander had visited Edinburgh, so Sadie's understandably nervous. I am too. That's why I've been up Scott Monument so much lately—to try and detect if he's lurking around.'

I'm talking to Damian as if he's one of us, and I know this information is probably difficult to comprehend, but he seems to be doing OK with it so far. Or so I think.

'Right. Um, exactly how old is Hester?' he asks slowly.

'Ah, she's from the mid-sixteenth century.'

Damian gapes. 'So like the Elizabethan era?' he chokes out.

I nod. 'Yes, she was turned in 1560, but we met her in 1921.'

A nerve in Damian's cheek twitches, and he lets out a slow breath. 'Jesus H. Christ,' he mutters. 'And Sadie? When did you meet her?'

'In 1921 as well, in Paris,' I say. 'But I'd been living there for thirty-three years before we ran into each other.'

'So what century is she from?'

'Eighteenth. She was turned in 1758.'

Damian rakes a hand through his hair, his face pale. 'And this guy, this vampire ex, that's after you for this thing you did—what about him?'

I shrug. 'He was always reluctant to tell me his age for some reason, even though I tried to pry it out of him numerous times. But he mentioned the original Globe Theatre a couple of times in passing, so he's at least as old as Hester. He's strong physically. And mentally, he can match all three of us put together, which ... Well, we're just lucky that Hester has her shielding ability that throws him off my scent.' I keep my tone light, but it's too late—

Damian's picked up on my hesitation.

'So I'm assuming Dryden is the vengeful, jealous type of vampire ex?'

'Yeah.'

'How much danger am I in?'

I hesitate, unsure how to respond without adding to his fear. But I have to tell him. 'Like all the blood sucked from your body and being ripped to shreds—that kind of danger.'

Damian's face turns ashen, and his eyes widen. He rubs at his temples with both hands, like he's having some kind of inner mental explosion.

Instantly, I'm in his lap and stroking his chest. 'Breathe, Damian, just breathe. It will be OK. We'll do everything in our power so that *won't* happen to you.'

He takes a deep shuddering breath, then another.

'OK. T-thank you,' he manages. 'I don't know why, but I do feel slightly more reassured by that.'

'De rien, ma chèrie.' Well, I didn't spend thirty-three years in Paris without picking up *some* French. I snuggle my face into the crook of his neck, and he puts his arms around me with a low murmur of satisfaction, as if he likes me being there. I cuddle him, transmitting some soothing energy as he processes this new information.

Eventually, Damian reaches the inevitable conclusion because he's a smart guy. 'So if you turn me into a vampire, he'll leave me alone? Is that the decision Sadie was talking about?'

I nod into his neck, hearing his pulse quicken. 'That's the theory. You'll be able to defend yourself at least, and from what I've experienced, newbies are strong. Plus with four against one, we've got a much better chance if he comes for us.'

'And if I don't want that?'

'Then we'll give you a memory wipe, including my dental appointment. You'll never know I exist,' I say, the words muffled against his chest.

Damian strokes my hair, and I resist the temptation to read his thoughts as he ponders this.

'It's a lot to think about,' he says at last, sounding rattled. 'I have a job and a family. I have a life. It's not a perfect life, but at least I know it's going to end at some point. I'm not sure I'd be able to handle living forever. It's just too hard to comprehend.'

I attempt to understand Damian's way of thinking, and I partly get it, but not entirely. My sense of forever is warped. Years race by in the blink of an eye; decades merge and clump together like raindrops sliding down a windowpane.

'What's to comprehend? The world changes, and as a vampire, you just change with it and adapt. It's not hard to do. You just get on with it,' I tell him stiffly. OK, I wasn't expecting him to jump for joy, but I'm hurt at my boyfriend's close-minded attitude. *Vengeful exes aside, wouldn't spending eternity with moi be at least a little bit fun?*

CHAPTER 29

Florence | Paris, 1921

Aunt Ivy is dying, but Alexander won't let me go back to London to visit her. I'm raging. The short family holiday has turned into thirty-three fucking years. By now, I've mentioned to her that I'm with Alexander, but I've never referred to him as my husband since he's certainly never got down on one knee. I've simply let her assume he is.

Aunt Ivy's letters to me are filled with resignation about her cancerous tumour and gentle understanding. After all, I must be terribly busy being a doctor's wife, and that's why I can't visit her. Otherwise, she knows I would. But I can read between the lines—she's hurt that I'm unable to, especially since she's on her deathbed and the war's been over for three years.

How can I tell her that my master is a controlling bullheaded vampire and he refuses to let me?

'Death is par for the course with humans. The sooner

you accept that, the better,' says Alexander impatiently when I ask him to let me leave Paris for the twentieth time. 'It's best if you stay away. It will just be too distressing for you.'

'I'm not a child, Alexander,' I reply through gritted teeth. 'And she's like a mother to me—you know that.'

'No, Florence,' he repeats, twitching his shirt cuffs as he prepares for a feeding jaunt. 'You will stay here. With me. And for God's sake, stop asking me about it. It's damned irritating.'

'Uncaring bastard!' I shout at him and run out of the room, wishing I could at least burst into tears.

Our fights seem to be getting worse. He's leaving the house at odd hours and avoiding eye contact whenever I ask him where he's going, which is making me highly suspicious about what he's up to.

Alexander's hold on me has weakened bit by bit over the years, and any love I once felt has been replaced with bitter resentment for being kept as an obedient pet. Only the well-stocked library and my secret nightly excursions console me. Through reading, I can escape, and Paris is breathtakingly beautiful at night. But it's lonely traversing the rooftops by myself, and I wish I had someone to share it with.

***

After our latest blow-up, I hide in the parlour until he's gone out. Then I quickly get changed, determined to find out what he's up to despite the risk of detection. Until now, I've been scared of what he would do if he found out I'd followed him, but tonight I'm angry enough not to care. He's drained me to the point of death several times over the years whenever I threatened to leave. He never lets me die. I'm always nursed back to health slowly and carefully. My powerful master wants to teach me a lesson about who's in control, but I suspect he doesn't let me die because he's secretly afraid of being lonely.

The long johns have been ditched years ago. My 'cat burglar outfit', as I call it, is a sleek form-fitting black suit of black wool jersey with a lightweight silk stocking mask. To all intents and purposes, I'm a shadow stealthily leaping from chimney to chimney across the Parisian rooftops.

Alexander's carriage is easy enough to track, even though he's had a ten-minute start on me. He's heading towards Montmartre. After about twenty minutes, the carriage stops outside a townhouse, and he checks both ways he steps out. I hide behind a chimney across the road in case he looks up, but he doesn't. Not once. His mind is obviously elsewhere, and I can sense that he's not attuned to me at this moment. As why would his duteous pet ever disobey him? She knows the consequences if she does.

From this vantage point, I can see directly into the third-floor bedroom. I don't have to wait too long before there's a flurry of a dark cloak, a sweep of red silk robes, ruby wine being poured. The curtains are drawn back with a gold tassel, and I've got a front-row seat to the licentious action.

Alexander is naked, bracing himself against the side of the bed, his head thrown back. Thanks to my excellent hearing, his ecstatic moans float clearly through the slightly open window as two beautiful dark-haired whores take turns sucking his cock.

I assume he'll feed from them before he lets it go any further. (It's annoying that he's letting them do that, but I suppose I can forgive him this discretion as he has to lure them in some way. And whores are cheap and easy pickings.)

But to my chagrin, he seems to have no intention of feeding—only to take his pleasure as much as he can. After a short interlude, where he delicately cleans his come off the whores' faces and breasts with a washcloth, everyone takes a little refreshment (well, they do).

The whores sip wine and nibble on cakes on the couch as Alexander moves between them on his knees, licking their nipples and nuzzling between their spread legs with much giggling and moaning going on. His cock must be getting stiff again as the ménage à trois moves to the bed. I gape as one whore glides onto his cock, and the other rides his face like a practised well-oiled machine.

It hits me then with utter certainty that this arrangement has been going on for quite some time while I've been stuck alone in the house by myself. And his familiarity with them suggests they're not random whores, but his mistresses. Human thralls that he's picked out because he liked the look of them and because I wasn't enough to keep him satisfied. They could be 40 years old but look 20 because Alexander's venom is keeping them young, fresh, and nubile for his evening enjoyment. My master is a cheating bastard!

***

Outraged and hurt at Alexander's betrayal, I roof-hop all the way back to the house, bellowing at the top of my lungs. The noise I'm making causes a fair few windows to be flung open and sleep-disturbed residents to poke their heads out and bawl 'Tais-toi!' into the street, thinking I'm a drunken reveller.

Back at home, I rip off my outfit and stuff it in the drawer and bash at the wardrobe door with my fist in a fit of rage. I'm going to have to come up with an excuse for the holes, but I'll worry about that later. Right now, I need ...

revenge.

Donning a slinky black flapper dress, fishnet stockings, high heels, and a jewelled headband, I stalk to the nearest bar, determined to get my own back. Although Alexander has taken me out on the town to feed occasionally in the last thirty-three years, he's always been the one to do the dirty work, so I'm at a loss as to how to flirt convincingly and attract a potential victim (preferably male and handsome). My come-hither looks are perceived as hostile glares, and all the men I target sidle hurriedly away.

After aimlessly wandering from club to club, I end up in a place called Harry's New York Bar. The bartender is chatty and friendly. He tells me to call him Pete. He's experimenting with a new drink featuring tomato juice and vodka that he calls a Bloody Mary and wants me to try it. I humour him with a few sips, but I wish he would put real blood in it. I'm about to count my losses and call it a night when there's a cold frisson in the air, and the back of my neck prickles. Slowly, I turn around and come face to face with an attractive young blonde woman. She's wearing a criminally short strappy green silk dress and an emerald-studded headband. That she's a vampire I'm in no doubt. Alexander has told me we're not the only ones in Paris, but this is the first time I've met one in the wild.

We eye each other silently, assessing who's the more

dangerous, and my fists slowly clench; if she's feeling territorial and wants to go outside, then I'm in the mood for a fight. The woman's lips quirk as if she's amused. This suggests she's not afraid of me at all, and I should be on my guard.

Then she holds up a hand like a peace offering and wiggles her fingers in greeting. There's a crackling in my mind, and her husky voice comes through loud and clear.

Hello, witch. Wanna have some fun?

***

Sadie, I'm not sure about this—

My new vampire friend has invited me to her apartment, where she said there's a treat in store for me. But I wasn't expecting a guy to be spreadeagled on her double bed, wearing nothing but a white towel. He's bound by invisible ropes to the bedposts, and it doesn't seem to be any effort on Sadie's part to hold him there. She's tied a black silk blindfold over his eyes, but by the sharp cut of his jaw, broad tanned chest, and rippling biceps, I can tell he's an Adonis in his birthday suit.

Sadie ignores my protest.

Meet Chad from the US of A. I forget which state. He did tell me.

'Where are you from again, Chad?' she asks out loud.

'Oklahoma,' he says in an American accent, jerking his head towards her voice.

Sadie snaps her fingers. *Right, that's it. He's an army lad, serving God and country. But most importantly, serving up ...*

She whips off the towel, and Chad's extremely large cock is displayed in all its erect glory.

Jesus!

Sadie grins at my reaction. *Isn't it delightful? Tastes even better.*

She dips her head, licking slowly up his impressive length. Chad lets out a soft moan and strains against the invisible ropes as she runs her tongue around the sensitive tip. My eyes widen as she proceeds to sink her teeth into his muscular upper thigh, sucks out a mouthful of blood, and drips it onto his cock. Part of me feels I should back quickly out of the room and leave them to it, but my eyes are glued to the scene, unable to look away.

Sadie takes her time, smearing blood along his length, then swirling around the tip with her finger. Chad starts writhing around in pleasure. 'Oh god,' he whimpers. 'Fuck me. Please fuck me, Sadie.'

Arousal erupts between my legs at the sight of his engorged member and bulging muscles, and my fangs spike out of my gums at the smell of his blood. Sadie glances at me and smirks, seeing that I'm drooling. *Chad's all yours if you want him. I fucked and sucked him two nights ago, and as you can see, he's up for it again. He's prime beef.*

She makes a silent kissing motion with her fingertips.

I hesitate. *I'm really not sure.*

She frowns. *You've just caught your boyfriend cheating on you with two thralls. You deserve some fun.*

She lifts Chad's spectacular ruby-red dripping cock and waggles it at me. He groans again, asking Sadie to fuck him and put him out of his misery. She grins.

What are you waiting for? No harm done, and Chad will love it. Just keep the blindfold on him, and he won't know it's not me. And don't worry, I won't tell anyone. Cross my heart and hope to die.

She winks at me, blows a kiss at Chad, and leaves silently before I can tell her that this is a big mistake.

Unaware that she's left, Chad begs again for Sadie to fuck him and juts his hips at me, obviously desperate for release.

Oh god, he is delectable.

Quietly, I slip out of my dress, stockings, and heels, then crawl naked onto the bed—fangs bared, eyes fixed on Chad's blood-smeared cock. Perhaps just a little taste ...

CHAPTER 30

Damian | Edinburgh, present day

I've said the wrong thing. I know Floss well enough by now to tell when she's upset. Her smooth forehead wrinkles slightly, and her eyes get this glazed sad look, like she's tormented and wishes she could cry. But I know she can't. There are things about being a vampire like that that really punch me in the gut. I'm not saying I want to bawl my eyes out if I'm sad, but it would be nice to have the option.

She gets up slowly from my lap and starts mindlessly rearranging ornaments on the sideboard.

'Floss ...'

'If you can't handle eternity with me, maybe we should call it quits now. I can get Hester to memory-wipe you this evening.' She says it jokingly, but her attitude riles me.

'I haven't decided anything yet. At least give me some time to think about it.'

Floss crosses her arms and looks at me. 'How much time

do you need? I would have thought it was kind of an easy decision. You know, since we slept together and since it was so "frigging magical",' she says, using air quotes.

Oh, so this is what she's upset about. She's annoyed that I have to think about becoming a vampire. That I'm not just automatically choosing her.

'Seriously? This is a huge decision. You've put me in an impossible position. I'm either spending eternity as a vampire or spending the rest of my life not knowing you exist? And why would you think I'd be happy about that?'

'Oh.' Floss looks at me warily, and I can tell she's dying to read my mind to find out how I feel about her.

I sigh. 'Just do it. It's not like I can keep any secrets from you anyway.'

She shakes her head.

I go over to her and put my arms around her, but it's like hugging a statue. I stroke her back, kiss her temple, but she refuses to budge. 'Just go, Damian.'

Floss mentioned her sire, Alexander, is stubborn. I'm beginning to see where she gets it from.

'I don't want to,' I murmur. 'I don't want to leave you like this.' Especially as now I'm worried she's going to get Hester to memory-wipe me anyway. I might wake up tomorrow, and knowing her will be nothing but a lovely dream. It puts things into startling perspective.

I do some eyebrow gymnastics to make her laugh and get a wan smile.

'Go home.'

'No. Read my thoughts.'

She shakes her head again.

'Please.'

She rolls her eyes. 'Fine.'

Don't make me live without you.

I tip up her chin and kiss her. It's a little like kissing an ice sculpture, but I persist until she finally opens her mouth with a little moan and lets me swirl in my tongue.

I want to be with you. It's a no-brainer.

Floss removes her lips from mine and stares at me. 'Don't think things you don't mean.'

'I do mean it, and I can prove it.'

'How?'

'Feed from me.'

CHAPTER 31

Florence | Edinburgh, present day

Damian's face is nervous as I spread several clean towels over the bed. 'Don't worry, I'm not about to waste a precious drop. It's just in case there's spillage.' Our dry-cleaner's have already been memory-wiped once this month, and I don't fancy washing my bedcover by hand.

'I trust you,' he says, and I nod, glad to hear it. Excitement and anticipation are thrilling through my veins that I get to taste him, to drink from him again.

We lie together on the bed in our underwear, Damian in his boxers and me in my loosened corset. He squeezes his eyes shut and tilts his head to one side, baring his neck, and I resist the urge to giggle. It's like we're re-enacting a scene out of a bad Dracula movie. Oh well, so be it.

I place a finger over the spot where I'll sink my fangs in and press lightly, feeling his heightened pulse drumming beneath my fingertips.

'Last chance. Are you sure you want me to do this?' My fangs are extended and aching to puncture his skin. I'm pretty sure I'll be able to stop before I drain him, but I have to ask. Maybe I should get him to sign a disclaimer? *I give Florence Hughes permission to suck on my neck and take full responsibility for the consequences ...*

'I want it,' Damian replies, his voice trembling slightly. 'Just make it quick.'

Before he can change his mind, I swoop in and latch on to his neck. Piercing through the skin and down into his throbbing jugular, I suck out a generous measure of his warm precious life. Damian moans and thrashes his legs as my venom hits his system. I lick the holes I've made with my tongue and suck some more. His heartbeat is going through the roof.

You taste divine, I tell him. *You OK?*

Yes, take more if you like.

I groan as another mouthful of his silky smooth blood hits the back of my throat, knowing that this is just the beginning and my thirst for him will never be satiated.

***

A few days after 'the feeding', Damian messages me at dusk.

Hey, do you want to come over? I'm making us dinner. Dxx

Interesting. What does that entail? Fxx

You'll find out. Dxx

Intrigued, I start getting ready. Is Damian going to serve me rare steak while he chomps on his own medium-rare piece? Unless he means *he's* the dinner, which would be even better. My mouth waters at the thought. His blood is tasty, and I can't wait to get my fangs into him yet again. Luckily, I managed to stop myself before draining him dry the other night, and he even said he enjoyed the experience after the initial biting part.

He seems to be coming round to the idea of being turned. I had a sneaky peek after I fed from him. His thoughts were full of wondering what it would be like to be immortal and, of course, how great it would be to hang out with moi for eternity and have lots of vampire sex (I may have subtly projected that thought into his mind).

However, we need to talk about it more as he wants to think through the practical side of it, especially in terms of his job and his family. It's true being a vampire is cool, but it's not all flying around in the moonlight and enjoying an ageless appearance. There are certain sacrifices you have to make. He might have to quit his job or become estranged from his family so they don't ask questions about why he's not ageing and why he's requesting rare roast beef for Sunday lunch.

And adding to our coven will mean Elliott will have another mouth to feed. We rely on him so heavily now as it is, and there are only so many donations per week that he can muster. But Damian can feed from me initially, so it's not a pressing problem.

As if she senses me thinking about Elliott, Sadie summons me just as I step out of my lair.

Sadie: *Can you bloodseek tonight?*

Me: *I'm literally about to go to Damian's.*

Sadie: *Can you do it afterwards?*

Me: *Not really.*

Sadie: *Fine. Just make sure you do it soon.*

She leaves my mindspace abruptly like someone slamming a door. *Wow, someone's feeling edgy tonight.*

For a minute, I feel bad. But I'm wearing my corset, fishnet stockings, and suspenders. It's sexy, but uncomfortable as hell to climb in.

***

'What exactly are you cooking?' I eye Damian's dining table suspiciously. He's set it for two, but there's no cutlery, only a red napkin and a white paper straw beside each place mat.

A couple of candles burn sultrily in brass holders.

'You'll find out in exactly'—he looks at his watch—'two minutes. Now if you would be so good as to take a seat, my lady.'

He pulls out the chair for me in a gentlemanly fashion, and I resist the urge to snort. It would be rude as he's gone to some effort to make it romantic and has even dressed up formally in a suit and tie. All rather strange for a Wednesday night, but I'll run with it.

He kisses the top of my head. 'I'll be back in a mo,' he murmurs. I tilt my chin up, wanting a proper kiss, but he's skedaddled back to the kitchen.

I sigh and fiddle with my straw.

A whirring noise sounds from the kitchen.

A clatter. Then swearing.

I giggle softly to myself. I get the impression Damian's not used to cooking.

He pokes his head out the doorway.

'If you would be so good as to close your eyes.'

Obediently, I shut my eyes as he places objects on the table and fusses around a bit.

'You can look now,' he says at last.

I crack open an eye to find a pint glass of red liquid sitting in front of me. It's decorated with a wedge of pineapple on the side, and several cocktail umbrellas have been poked in. A familiar heavenly aroma wafts upward, and I lean forward and sniff.

'Is this ...?'

Damian smirks and nods, looking pleased with himself.

He sits across the table with the same ruby-red drink festooned with decorations in front of him. He plonks in the straw and bends down to place it to his lips.

Dismay rolls through me.

'Damian, please don't—'

But he takes a long suck before I can stop him. I gape as he licks his lips. Surely, he can't think it tastes good! He laughs at my expression of horror.

'Mine's tomato gazpacho.'

'Oh.' I laugh in relief. 'You had me worried for a minute there.'

'Drink up,' he urges.

I take a sip. The blood is warm and velvety smooth and slides down my throat like tangy molasses. I groan aloud.

'Oh my god, this is perfect. But it tastes like you ...?'

Damian grins. 'I had a little help from Elliott. I said I wanted to make you a surprise dinner, and he took a donation from me after work and stayed for a coffee.'

Those two are getting along like a house on fire. I suck up another mouthful of blood, watching Damian through narrowed eyes. 'Should I be worried about this budding bromance of yours?'

He frowns. 'It's not like that. He's cool. But it's more about having a human to chat to, especially at the flat. Having him there makes me feel less nervous, especially with Sadie constantly staring at my neck.'

Oh dear. Well, he's going to have to know at some point. 'Elliott isn't actually all human,' I say slowly.

Damian pauses midsuck. '*What*?'

'He's a thrall—Sadie's thrall, to be exact. They've been together since 1983.'

A droplet of red gazpacho lands on the white tablecloth from Damian's abandoned straw. But it's not a good time to mention it. His eyes are round. 'What's a "thrall"? I mean, I know generally what it is. But how does it work here?'

'She keeps him on a leash. Well, not literally. But when she clicks her fingers, he jumps. Hester and I don't like the way she treats him, and we've tried talking to her about it, telling her to turn him. But she won't listen.' I shrug helplessly. 'She seems to like the control. Perhaps she's worried if she does, he'll start lording it over her. She hasn't had good experiences with men in her life. So I understand it, but I still feel sorry for Elliott.'

I know I'm sharing too much, but Damian seems to have recovered remarkably well and is listening without freaking out, which is a good sign.

'So Elliott's literally stuck in the 1980s?' he asks.

I nod.

'Wow, his obsession with Duran Duran now makes a lot more sense.'

'Yeah. He was their roadie when they became famous, so understandably, he's a big fan ...'

I didn't think I could blow Damian's mind, but by the way his jaw slackens and his eyes glaze over, I think I just have.

He drags a hand across his face. 'Fuck me sideways.'

I finish my drink with a flourishing slurp to change the subject.

'That was delicious, thanks.'

But Damian's frowning and looking anxious.

'I don't want to be a thrall,' he blurts out. 'If you turn me, I want you to do it properly. I don't want to be stuck in limbo like Elliott.'

Oh, so that's what he's worried about. I take his hand and squeeze it. 'I will. I'm not Sadie. Besides, you're not suddenly going to start ordering me around just because you're a male vampire. I don't think we work like that. Our dynamic feels different.'

Damian nods. 'I can't say what I would or wouldn't do because I don't know. But if I do start acting like a dick, just bite me and tell me not to be an arsehole.'

I giggle at that.

'Um, also, can you explain a bit more about how ... how turning someone works exactly?' he asks, his cheeks flushing the same shade as his half-finished gazpacho.

I know he's been dwelling on this a lot (and watching lots of vampire movies), and I want to put him out of his misery—or give him something to look forward to.

'Hmm ... So I'd suck your neck to the point of death, then give you my blood to drink. Once you transitioned and woke up, we'd make love and feed from each other. The transition will be a bit uncomfortable. But afterwards ... Well, let's just say it's an extremely pleasurable experience— ten times better than human sex,' I say nonchalantly, inspecting my newly painted purple nails.

There's a long silence.

I glance up to see that Damian's pupils are dilated, and he's chewing on his bottom lip. I can scent his arousal from here.

I smile to myself.

It doesn't take much to get him going, and I'm not complaining. But I won't be turning him tonight. I want to enjoy him as a human a little bit longer.

CHAPTER 32

Florence | Paris, 1921

After the Chad incident, I start keeping company with Sadie Bouffant. She told me her original name was Sadie Smith, but since she's been working as a high-class prostitute in Paris, she thought she needed a fancier surname. Being with Sadie is a lot more fun than staying home alone, plus she's skilled at enticing good-looking Americans to drop their trousers.

Of course, Alexander is livid that I'm out most nights and makes a lot of threats to keep me inside. But as he's not willing to stop his 'diversions', I don't care what he says anymore. I'm having too much fun being footloose and fancy-free. Besides, Sadie's right: I can't rely on Alexander as my food source forever. I need to learn how to feed sustainably if I want to be independent.

However, one night, he loses his cool completely when I'm getting dressed to go out dancing.

'I forbid you to go anywhere with that whore!' he howls, ripping at the bedsheets with his nails.

I ignore him. 'Sadie's not a whore,' I lie, putting on dark-purple lipstick, my new favourite colour.

'She is a *literal* whore! A Covent Garden prostitute from the 1750s!'

I narrow my eyes, suspicious at the specific decade he's used.

'How do you know that?'

'I asked around. She's not the sort of company you should be keeping!'

Rip, rip, rip go the bedsheets as Alexander works himself into a frenzy.

I roll my eyes at his childish tantrum and search for my beaded purse instead. *I'm sure I hung it up in the wardrobe … Ah, there it is.*

'Florence, are you listening to me?'

I sigh and face him. 'I don't care what Sadie does for a living, Alexander. She's my friend, and I like her. She's fun.'

'But you have *me*. I'm fun!' he yowls, the bedsheets now completely shredded into ribbons.

Yes, I have you in some capacity—when you can be bothered. But honestly, it's not enough.

***

'You should leave him,' says Sadie when I get to the club

and complain about Alexander. We're sucking on a couple of 'special' Bloody Marys, thanks to Sadie's hip flask.

I toy with my chin-length bobbed hair, which is the reason for my latest fight with Alexander. He likes my hair long and was furious that I cut it off.

'He said if I leave, he'll find me and snap my neck.'

'Having one's neck snapped is better than living in prison,' Sadie counters.

'I'm here with you now, aren't I?'

'Until Alexander binds you to the bedpost.'

'He wouldn't dare,' I scoff but feel a little uneasy.

'If you say so. Ooh, hello, what do we have here?'

A good-looking marine saunters past, checking us out. Sadie cocks her head, keeping her eyes trained on him as he nudges his three equally attractive friends, and they look us over. She licks her lips.

Sadie: *Those four are adorably juicy. Shall we?*

Me: *Four at once! That's going a bit far.*

Sadie: *Oh, go on, live a little. What's good for the goose is good for the gander and all that. It'll be fun, an all-you-can-eat man buffet.*

Me (laughing): *All right, you know I can never resist a man in uniform—*

Sadie: *Or several of them out of it.*

***

The next week, I'm back at the club, raging after another fight with Alexander. Sadie rolls her eyes.

'Leave him, Floss.'

I take a sip of my Bloody Mary.

'I *am* seriously considering it,' I tell her.

'You say that, but chances are we'll be having this same conversation in twenty years' time,' she replies, adjusting her headband. I bristle at her confident tone and the fact that she's probably right.

Dammit.

'You think I won't?'

'I know you won't, little puppet.'

The desire to prove her wrong burns in my chest.

I lift my chin. 'I'll have you know I've got a plan.'

Sadie looks at me in mock amazement. 'You have?'

'Yes, I've got a secret suitcase packed. I'm going to escape to London one night when he's visiting his whores. There's a train from Gare du Nord that departs at seven and reaches Calais at midnight to connect with the last ferry crossing to Dover.'

'And then?'

'Then ... then ...' My voice falters. 'That's as far as I've got.'

Sadie snorts.

'That's not much of a plan. You're going to need money for a start. Otherwise, you'll end up in the tunnels of the London Underground, feeding on rats.'

I shudder. 'That's not a pleasant thought.'

'Isn't Alexander loaded?'

I nod. 'Apparently.'

'In that case, can't you nick some of it? If he's got plenty, he'd be none the wiser.'

'Nick it?' I echo, horrified as if the thought has never entered my head. In fact, I've been thinking the same thing for weeks. It's the missing piece of the puzzle. I refuse to work as a housemaid just because I need a lair of my own.

'Yes, nick it,' says Sadie patiently. 'It's not really stealing. It's compensation. You deserve it after what he's done to you.'

'That's true. And he got really nasty when I told him I knew about his French whores.'

'What happened?'

'He laughed in my face and told me to keep my nose out of his business. That he could fuck who he liked.'

'Arsehole,' says Sadie, looking murderous. 'I hope you told him that you'd fucked and feasted on four marines? And had a grand old time doing it?'

'Yes, I did. But ...' I rub at my cheek where Alexander hit

me. It's still a bit tender, even though the bruising healed pretty much instantly.

'Bastard,' Sadie spits. 'Where does he keep his chequebook and his account details?'

'In the safe,' I reply.

'Do you know the code?'

I shake my head. 'But I can try out some combinations.'

'Do it,' she urges. 'Because if you don't leave him, I'm going to have to drive a stake through his goddamn heart. And I'd rather not have another vampire's blood on my conscience.'

***

I prepare to make my escape from Alexander. When he's asleep, I practise forging his signature and try out different combinations on his safe. Because what other choice do I have? I mostly keep my head down and try not to make waves, even though he taunts and insults me and jeeringly asks if I want to join in with his ménage à trois. I would rather cut my own throat. But I grit my teeth, smile politely, and say, 'No thank you, dear.'

It takes a month and myriad combinations, but one Tuesday afternoon, I finally crack it. Turns out Alexander is a sentimental old fool—the code is the date he turned me:

03-10-1888. It will be his downfall.

Dressed to the nines in Sadie's fur and dripping with cheap jewellery, I saunter into the bank and claim to be Alexander's devoted wife, explaining that we need the funds to buy a townhouse for our daughter. But alas, my poor husband is ill and has sent me along in his stead. Aunt Ivy has taught me well when it comes to faking documents. I hand over a signed letter from Alexander duly giving me permission to withdraw his funds and requesting to please make the cheque out to his wife as she will be handling the purchase. It's a performance I'm particularly proud of. By the time I leave, I've cleaned out half of his Paris account, walking away with a cheque for 200,000 francs made out in my name. They don't even question why my name is Florence Hughes instead of Florence Dryden.

Sadie is so impressed by this that she decides to come with me once I promise her a share in the money. It's a fresh start for her too as she wants to give up prostitution.

We slip out of France by train and ferry, bound for London. Once there, we open a joint business account at Lloyds, saying we're thinking of running a Parisian-style tea room. We act posh and charming so the clerk doesn't ask too many questions or look too closely at the fake IDs Sadie's rustled up for us. After depositing the money, we rent a modest room in Bayswater. As Sadie wisely puts it,

'Alexander's money needs to last us for decades, if not centuries, so there's no point squandering it on fancy hotels from the start.'

Sadie is a powerful vampire, but even she knows she's done for if Alexander tracks us down.

However, that's something we've factored into the equation. Our plan is to keep moving and always be one step ahead of him. Since Alexander and I have a blood bond, I can sense him keenly if he's anywhere near me. We're hoping he eventually gets bored and leaves me alone.

However, realistically, this could take a while—depending on how long he nurses his grudge.

Still, we have time. And I'm free from his control for the first time in nearly thirty-five years, and that makes it worth the risk. Besides, as Sadie says, 'Two undead heads are better than one.'

We spend the nights practising sustainable feeding in the back alleys. Sadie is careful to memory-wipe our victims afterwards while I keep an eye out for anyone who looks suspiciously like a thrall.

But one day, I jerk awake from a nightmare where I'm running down a dimly lit street with Alexander hot on my heels. There's a tugging sensation in my chest, and my head is pounding with the force of his anger. A cold dread creeps over me.

Quickly, I wake Sadie and tell her Alexander is close by and that we need to leave *now*. We throw our things into our suitcases and silently slip out the back entrance of the guest house. Sprinting to the nearest Underground station, we disappear into the labyrinth of dark tunnels, making sure no one notices us. We go deeper and deeper until I can't feel him anymore.

That was too close for comfort.

And Sadie isn't happy about our new accommodation since it's sooty, smelly, noisy, and, in her words, 'not exactly the Ritz'.

'Fucking hell,' she complains two days later, ripping open the neck of an inordinately large water rat for us to feed on. 'This is just what I *didn't* want to happen.'

I'm not happy about it either, but what else can we do?

After five days, when the threat of Alexander discovering our whereabouts has entirely dissipated (as has most of the rat population), Sadie puts her foot down. 'We can't live like this—we need a proper plan.'

'Maybe Charlie can help us.'

She blinks at me in the violet light. 'Alexander's son?'

I nod.

'I thought he hated you?'

'He might be more accommodating now that I'm not with Alexander. Plus the fact that his papa hasn't been back to London to visit him could work in our favour—namely Alexander won't go near the house if Charlie doesn't like him very much.'

'Is he cute?'

'Very,' I say with a smile, and Sadie grins.

'What are his abilities?'

I shrug. 'Not sure. He didn't seem to have anything in particular, and his mental powers were kind of weak. Maybe they've developed since I last saw him, though.'

'I guess we'll find out. Hopefully, Charlie doesn't mind us smearing soot all over his furniture.'

CHAPTER 33

Damian | Edinburgh, present day

I don't normally see patients during my lunch hour, but this is a special check-up—one that requires locking the door of my exam room.

Floss is lying back in my chair. She's naked apart from combat boots and a black lace bra that barely contains her breasts. Thanks to us making out as soon as she arrived, I've got a hard-on the size of Krakatoa in my trousers.

I clear my throat, straighten my white coat, and pull up a chair, attempting not to stare between her thighs (it's a struggle). 'Now which teeth are causing you problems, Miss Hughes?'

'These ones, Doctor,' she says, opening her mouth and pointing to her canines, which have extended as she's been licking my neck. They tend to come down automatically when she's experiencing 'bloodlust'—a combination of intense horniness and an overwhelming urge to drink my blood (she says I'll find out what it's like if I decide to get turned). Part of me is very curious, but I can't imagine having fangs or wanting to bite people with them. Also, a vampire dentist who sucks his patients' blood wouldn't have the greatest retention rate. So there's that.

Yet Floss's fangs are infinitely fascinating, and I've found myself in a number of potentially dangerous situations lately involving them. But then again, as Floss says, she's quite able to suck my cock without biting it off. So far, that's been true.

'Ah, I see,' I say, lifting back her upper lip. Her fangs are snowy white, curved, and look razor-sharp. 'Are they painful?'

Floss hisses a laugh. 'Only if you get too close, Doctor.'

'Hmm,' I say, bending to press my lips against the tops of her voluptuous breasts. I push down her bra and free her dusky-pink nipples, twirling one, then the other with my tongue. 'Is this too close?'

'I think you're fine,' Floss murmurs. I trail a hand down over her pale midriff, then lower to gently caress her pussy.

'What about now?'

She groans softly. 'I came here for a fang check-up, Doctor, not a gynaecological exam.'

'Why not both?' I quip, lightly circling her clit. 'I can multitask.'

'That's very clever of you,' she says, her voice sounding slightly strangled as I rub her clit with my index finger.

Fuck, that feels good, Dr Rhodes.

I grin. I love it when she talks to me in my mind; it feels so intimate. I only wish I could hear what she's thinking ... Perhaps one day. For now, I'm happy enough that she can pick up on my thoughts.

As my cock has been released from my pants—when did that happen?—and Floss is stroking it, it means she has indeed read my thoughts. I sigh in pleasure as her fingers twirl around the juicy tip and slide up and down, firm, the way I like it. The coldness of her fist does nothing to temper my burning desire. *Thank you,* I think to her. *The rest of the afternoon was going to be difficult with that monster in my trousers.*

I can tame your monster. Floss pokes the tip of her tongue out at me and wiggles it. I swallow hard. As much as I want her to give me a blow job right now, the logistics are too difficult.

That's OK. I can wait—

She cuts me off, insisting, *Don't be silly. Swap places.*

Somehow, I end up lying on my own dentist chair, still in my white coat, with my trousers around my thighs and Floss working my cock into a frenzy with her lips and tongue. She seems to be half hovering on top of me. I can't quite tell as I'm writhing around in rapture and trying not to moan too loudly in case my receptionist wonders what's going on in here. Floss sucks my entire length into her throat and does some complicated licking thing. Her fangs graze the edges of my cock. It's painful, but immensely pleasurable too. She knows exactly how to make my hips buck and balls tighten.

Ahhh, orgasm imminent. Just a heads-up, I warn.

Excellent, thanks. I sense her amusement.

Her lips clamp around my base, sucking hard. With a low moan, I offload what feels like a bucketload of come down her throat. Floss eagerly gulps every last drop and licks me clean. Afterwards, I lie on the chair, dazed, with my legs splayed, breathing heavily.

Jesus H. Christ, that was incredible, I think as Floss strokes my sweaty brow and kisses my cheek.

You needed that. You work too hard.

'Can you visit me every lunch hour?' I say out loud and only half-jokingly.

'Sure.' She smiles contentedly.

But I'm worried that I've been a selfish boyfriend. That I've taken my pleasure and left her hanging.

'Did you ...?'

'No. Close, but no,' she whispers in my ear. 'But it's OK. I wanted to take care of you.'

The alarm on my phone goes off, signalling that my next patient is due in five minutes.

I drag my hand over my face, attempting to stay awake.

All I want to do is take Floss home, give her pussy a thorough licking, and fall asleep with her in my arms. But I can't.

'Shit, I've got a root canal.'

Floss nods and helps me off the chair. She pulls up my briefs and trousers and buttons my coat. Then she adjusts her bra and quickly dons her long black ruffled skirt and prim high-necked blouse and overcoat.

'Catch you later, Dr Rhodes.' She winks and blows me a kiss as she glides towards the door—oh no, she's leaving before I've had a chance to ...

'I love you.' The words come tumbling out of my mouth before I can stop them.

Floss halts in her tracks and turns to look at me. Her violet eyes gleam. *What?*

I turn away, my hand shaking, as I tidy my already carefully arranged instruments on the tray.

I know I probably shouldn't say that. It's making my decision even harder. But I can't help how I feel. It's silly.

In a flash, she's in front of me, peering into my face.

It's not silly, Damian. I love you too.

I gaze at her. *Really?*

She grins and hugs me. *Of course I do. It was love at first bite. I fell for you head over heels when you came round to mine, after our date at The Brief Encounter.*

I frown, confused. *First bite? But I didn't come round after, and you didn't …*

Uh, yes. I did. She pulls back and looks at me guiltily. *You won't remember as I gave you a teensy, tiny memory wipe. But don't worry, we had a fun time, and you tasted delicious.*

CHAPTER 34

Florence | London, 1921

When Charlie opens the door to us in Belgravia, he's changed so much that I can't believe it's the same person—until he opens his mouth and says with a sneer, 'I knew you'd come crawling back one day, wench.'

I gaze at him in shock. 'What happened to you?'

Charlie's jaunty youthful looks have vanished. Standing before me is a middle-aged man in a stained cardigan with a paunch and a lined crotchety face.

'Have you been drinking bad blood or something?'

He scowls. 'You always did have such delightful manners, bitch. You'd better come in. Your friend too.' Charlie waves us inside, and cautiously, we follow him down the dim hallway to the parlour.

It's so strange being back in this gloomy house. Everything looks exactly the same, like I've stepped into a time capsule. I almost expect Alexander to be in his study like the old days. But I push away the feelings of regret for my past life before they overwhelm me; this is neither the time nor place for nostalgia.

Charlie gestures for us to sit on the emerald-green couch. He frowns as Sadie shakes her skirt out, and a cloud of soot rises into the air.

'Sorry, we're a bit dirty,' I say hastily. 'We've been staying in the Underground.'

He sniggers. 'Can't afford a hotel?'

Sadie tilts her head slightly at me. *Don't say anything about the money! I've blocked him so he can't hear us.*

'Something like that, Charlie,' I say smoothly as we settle on the couch, trying not to dislodge any more soot. 'Just saving our pennies at the moment. London accommodation has become more expensive since the war.'

'Well, you can't stay here,' he says grumpily, staggering to an armchair and lowering himself into it as if his knees hurt.

I thought you said he was cute? And I've discovered what his power is—being an arthritic arsehole!

I bite back a laugh.

'Are you actually still a vampire?' I ask him curiously. 'You look a lot older, which is very odd.'

Charlie's nostrils flare white at the edges. He leans forward slightly and hisses. 'Papa gave me something before you left for Paris. He said it was to help me sleep, but it seems to have kick-started my ageing process.'

'What the fuck?' says Sadie incredulously. 'Is that even possible?'

Charlie bares his fangs at her. 'Apparently. But as you can see, I'm still a vampire—just a decrepit one. Which is making it fucking difficult to attract the pretty whores. Oh yes, they all wanted handsome young Charlie,' he says bitterly. 'For years, I tasted their delicious blood and fucked their lush pussies. Now I'm left with the middle-aged gin harlots with sagging tits and dried-up cunnies.'

I glance at Sadie, and she's trying not to laugh.

'I don't even know why I call Dryden "Papa",' Charlie continues, clenching his fists. 'He's not my real father.'

'Oh?' I say, interested to hear that.

'No, he latched on to Mama after my real father died and decided to turn both of us into vampires to create himself a happy undead family when I was in my twenties. But he did something to Mama—I don't know what—and she died. So he was lumped with me. If he ever comes back here, I'll cut off his cock and shove it down his throat for what he's done to me. I *loathe* him!'

Sadie and I stare at seething Charlie, his face all twisted with rage, then at each other.

Sadie: *You were right. He's got a vendetta. Seems your charming sire has made another enemy.*

Me: *Let's make it work for us.*

Sadie: *Tread carefully. Act sympathetic.*

'I'm so sorry, Charlie,' I say. 'That is truly appalling that Alexander did that to you. As you might have guessed, I've left him because I couldn't stand the way he was controlling me. But since we're here, maybe we could team up and help each other out?'

Good, Floss. Let him know he can trust us.

But Charlie looks at me suspiciously after this little speech even though I've said it as genuinely as possible. Then he seems to consider the practicalities of us being there.

'Perhaps we could,' he says after a moment. 'Some vampire blood might help me recover. But what can I do for you?'

'We need protection, a way of making sure that Alexander can't track Floss,' Sadie says.

Charlie stares at me. 'You're blood-bonded, though. He'll always be able to find you, just like he can find me.'

Great, we're going to be ripped to shreds, I groan to Sadie.

'*But*', Charlie continues, 'I do know someone who might be able to help. An older vampire. Hester Everill. I believe she can shield, though I never saw her do it. I ran with her back in the early 1900s, and we had a lot of fun tearing up the town—and each other.' Charlie waggles his eyebrows.

'That is, until I started falling apart. Then she dumped me like a hot potato.' He scowls. 'Come to think of it, she's a bitch, and I hate her guts.'

'Oh no!' we chorus.

'Please, Charlie, just tell us where she is. And we'll both give you a drink,' I plead.

He licks his lips. 'Well, last I heard she was moving to Edinburgh. Said London wasn't big enough for the both of us. But as I say, that was a couple of decades ago now. She might not even be there.'

'Whereabouts in Edinburgh?' Sadie enquires.

He shrugs. 'How should I know? But it shouldn't be too hard to find her. And you can't miss her: tall, red hair, green eyes—a pretty piece of pussy.' He smacks his lips. Sadie growls at him, and Charlie looks slightly disconcerted.

Sadie: *I'm starting to change my mind about giving him blood ...*

Me: *Relax. He's given us what we need. All we have to do is let him have a drink, head to Edinburgh, and locate this Hester Everill.*

Sadie: *I hope she wants a couple of cool unholy friends.*

***

'I can't believe that arsehole,' Sadie grumbles, yanking the curtain across the window so the first-class carriage is dimmed. She leans back against the headrest, rubbing her wrists, which have healed but still bear the imprint of Charlie's fang marks. He decided that two feeds from Sadie and one feed from me would be a fair trade for giving us the information about Hester.

'I suppose we should be grateful he didn't want to fuck us too.'

'Yes, we should be,' I tell her, rubbing my own wrist and putting my boots up on the empty opposite seat. 'We got off lightly, and now we have what we need.'

The carriage sways, and my hand rests protectively on the suitcase of Alexander's money lying between us. It's a mere drop in the ocean of what's in our London bank account, but it will set us up nicely in Edinburgh.

'It's been over twenty years since Charlie last saw her. This Hester woman may not even be in Edinburgh. And if she is, why would she help us?' Sadie says, putting her boots up next to mine. We'll be told off if the conductor catches us and be given the 'Ladies, don't do that please' speech. But I don't feel much like a lady anymore, and I'm sick of men telling me what to do.

'We have to try. Otherwise, we're going to be running from Alexander for a good while longer. He's really angry at me.'

Sadie grunts, 'You should have staked him.'

'I told you, I couldn't,' I reply tersely. She pats my arm, knowing that it's a subject that causes me angst.

'All right. I don't blame you.'

It's one thing to get rid of a serial killer terrorising Whitechapel, but quite another to murder my own master, even if the intention is there. I haven't forgiven him for not letting me go to Aunt Ivy on her deathbed, and I never will.

I visited her gravestone in Spitalfields before we left London and laid a red rose on it. Then I gave into my tearless grief as Sadie waited for me by the gate, giving me privacy.

Oh, Aunt Ivy, how could you have sent me to that man? I wish I'd refused to go and stayed with you.

Our conversation back in 1888 flits into my mind as it has been lately, and I smile wryly. She was so adamant that the job was going to be the making of me. Now here I am, immortal and on the run with a vampire friend.

I glance at Sadie, who still has her hand on my arm. But her eyes are closed, dark lashes fanning her pale cheeks: she's resting, preparing for whatever lies ahead when we reach Edinburgh because we're going to have to find accommodation and then feed.

No one would believe this is my life if I told them.

Maybe I should write a memoir and pretend it's fiction? I muse. My Life in Blood—*an innocent girl turned against her will by an evil vampire doctor. I could be the next Bram Stoker.* Grinning to myself, I drum my fingers softly on the suitcase and attempt to come up with a cracking first line as the train snakes onwards to Scotland.

CHAPTER 35

Florence | Edinburgh, present day

Fortunately, Damian didn't seem to mind that I sucked his blood and gave him a partial memory wipe when we first met. But we couldn't discuss it further as his root canal appointment was nigh. Pity we got cut short as I was still feeling in the mood after my almost orgasm. But he kissed me hard on the lips before I left his exam room and said he'd message me after work. Plus he said 'I love you' again and shot me a misty-eyed look before he started disinfecting his chair. Feeling on top of the world, I practically skipped home to do some work on my memoir.

I'm thinking of wrapping it up as it's getting lengthy. Not surprising when I've been working on it for over a century. On my last word count check, it was nearing 700,000, which is more than *War and Peace*.

I guess I've had a lot to say for myself, but I think it makes for good reading. I would like to give myself a happy ending (for the book, not the other kind!) so I'll need to write Damian into it. I've been thinking of adding him in as a modern Dickensian-type character called Dimpleton Rinks because he does have such a cute dimple when he smiles ...

Twenty minutes later, I get back to writing after having had a lovely daydream about Dimpleton Rinks doing naughty things to me with his large cock. I don't think the story will suffer if I add in some more erotic scenes. Sex sells, as they say.

I'll let Hester read it and see what she thinks. She likes spicy romances. Sadie's not much of a reader; she prefers audiobooks, but she's welcome to read it too if she wants since she's in it from 1921 onwards.

I know her, though; she'll want me to change it if she doesn't agree with how I've portrayed her. But I reserve my right as the author to write anything I damn well want, even if it offends her delicate sensibilities. Hmm, I might not let her read it after all.

My phone lights up with a invite from Damian to come to his for a movie. I smile to myself. Last time I went round, there wasn't much movie watching happening.

***

Three hours later, I'm heading home, my pussy throbbing pleasantly. We began a movie, but the good doctor wanted to christen his new bed. And who was I to say no? Besides, it was another vampire movie, and I've seen them all.

Damian said I could sleep over, but I know he's tired after a busy day at work. So I stayed with him until he fell asleep, rubbing circles on his back.

I'm walking down the road to the bus stop and recalling the evening when my solar plexus starts pulsating madly. It could be because I've been thinking about Damian naked, but I know it isn't.

Oh no. Not here, not now!

Out of the corner of my eye, a sleek black car keeps pace with me, and I start walking faster. I try not to look at it and keep moving, but the tugging sensation worsens.

A low throaty chuckle emits from my right, and I turn my head slightly to see the tinted window has been lowered.

'Hello, Florence. Still looking as lovely as ever, my beauty. Even after a century.' Alexander's amused voice floats from the depths of the pitch-black car. I can't see him, but the scent of roses wafts from the open window. The smell of death and fear.

I walk faster, fists clenched, purple spots pricking the edges of my vision.

'Leave me alone!'

'No, my love. You knew there would be consequences for your actions. Too bad you won't get to say goodbye to that mortal you've been toying with. But it never would have worked out anyway.'

The car pulls to a stop and in one blink I'm next to it, reaching for the door handle against my will.

'Get in. You and I are going for a drive.'

Oh fuck, I'm going to die tonight ... and then he's coming back for Damian.

Alexander huffs a laugh. 'You always were astute, my darling.'

No, I can't let him kill me—I have to rescue Damian.

The thought of my lovely boyfriend being ripped to shreds by this monster jerks me out the stupor he's put me in. I yank my hand away from the car door as if it's burning.

'Fuck *off*!' I scream, backing away so quickly that I nearly knock over an older lady walking a poodle.

'Is he harassing you, dear? Bloody perv, I'll take care of him.' Whipping out her phone she punches in 999. 'Police please.' She walks around to the front of the car to read off his number plate in a loud voice causing Alexander to growl in annoyance. The poodle is barking and going nuts, so I don't wait around, and sprint back to Damian's flat. Phew, saved by a vigilant dog walker!

It's stupid and reckless as anyone could see me, but I choose a darkened spot at least and clamber up to the roof—not an easy feat in a long skirt and a corset. Lowering myself to the top-floor apartment, I bang on the window.

A sleepy Damian, wearing a T-shirt and boxers, heaves it up. 'Hey, did you forget—'

'No time to explain. Emergency.'

Before he can protest, I've reached in, plucked him from the room, and flown off towards the Old Town. We're cheek to cheek with his arms looped around my neck and my arms gripping tightly around his waist. Damian's shocked breath rasps in my ear, and his galloping heart is making it difficult for me to concentrate.

But I need to as I've only ever flown with Sadie. We were practising one night in case we needed to get away quickly from Alexander, and I dropped her. She landed on her feet in a graveyard, but she kept harping on about it for years afterward.

Keep as still as possible, I tell him nervously. *And close your eyes if you're afraid of heights.*

Damian obediently squeezes his eyes shut, but his body is quivering in terror as I shoot up to the cloud cover. A low moan escapes his mouth as the frigid winter air rushes over his extremities. I need to fly fast so he doesn't get hypothermia.

I attempt to connect with Sadie, but as per usual, she's blocking me. This time, it could be to her detriment.

Hester!

Hester!

Hester!

Screaming her name over and over in my mind is my only option, since I can't project thoughts to her, but luckily it seems to work.

Hester: *You OK? What's wrong?*

Me: *Thank God you heard me. I just bumped into Alexander, and I can't reach Sadie. Can you get back to the flat pronto? We need to check on her.*

Hester: *Fuck! I'm just heading back from my acting class. I'll be there in five.*

Panicking, I fly as fast as I can to Ramsay Garden with Alexander's damned nursery rhyme—'Ladybird, ladybird, fly away home'—and his maniacal laugh ringing in my head.

If he's hurt Sadie, I'll rip his head off ...

Damian shudders in my arms, and I realise I've said it in his mind.

I drop us outside the front door, and Damian sags against the railing, white-faced. But there's no time to comfort him.

Hester appears beside me in a flash.

'Quickly, get him inside,' she says, and we whisk Damian through the front door. I relax slightly.

Apart from Damian's hoarse breathing, the house is silent and in darkness.

'Sadie?' I call out.

There's no answer.

Hester: *Did she go out?*

Me: *No, Elliott was coming over.*

She jerks her chin towards the staircase.

Hester: *They must be in her room. We should check on them, just in case.*

I nod and slide my hand into Damian's sweaty one and tug him towards the staircase. I don't particularly want him to witness whatever's happening between Sadie and Elliott in her room. But I can't leave him alone either as he's scared out of his wits, he can't see, and I still haven't explained what's happening.

I bumped into Alexander down the road from your flat, I tell him as we climb the stairs to the top floor.

He squeezes my hand and lets out a breath.

I figured it was something like that.

I add, *We're checking up on Sadie and Elliott.*

He nods. *OK.*

I kiss his hand. *Don't worry, I'm sure they're fine. We've been pretty good at evading him so far.*

However, this changes things a lot. Alexander knows about us. So Damian's options are now 'be turned' or 'die', which is hardly a choice in the scheme of things.

We reach Sadie's door and listen, but there's no sound or movement.

Me: *Can you detect her in there?*

Hester: *Yes.*

Me: *Is she alive?*

Hester: *Yes.*

I squeeze Damian's hand in relief.

Me: *She's in there. And alive.*

Damian: *Thank goodness!*

Me: *Yes. Luckily, it wasn't a major disaster. But you should stay here with us for now so we can protect you.*

Damian nods, and I sense his fear return full force at what that means.

Wanting to see Sadie with my own eyes, I knock on the door and turn the handle, which opens easily. Her bedroom is set into the eaves of the roof, so the ceiling is vaulted. With my night vision, I spy the top of her blonde head over by the bed. She's sitting on the floor.

However, Damian can't see. So I reach out to switch on the lights.

Hester: *Wait, Floss, I don't think you should turn on the—*

But it's too late. Soft yellow floods the room, and I hurry to the other side of the bed and let out a gasp.

Sadie is covered in blood; her eyes are closed, and her mouth is open in a kind of silent scream. She seems to be paralysed.

Me: *Keep Damian back. Something's wrong.*

Hester: *What is it?*

Me: *I don't know. She's in shock.*

I crouch next to her and grasp her shoulder gently.

'Sadie? Are you hurt?'

Her eyes open, and she lets out a thin caterwaul, which causes the hairs on the back of my neck to rise.

Sadie: *Alexander's taken Elliott. He attacked him right in front of me! This is Elliott's blood, not mine.*

Hester: *Oh my god, how did he even enter without being invited?*

Sadie: *He broke in through Floss's entrance.*

Me: *What the fuck? How?*

Hester: *The blood bond may have given him right of entry. He was waiting for you to get back, Floss, so he could—*

She gives a sharp tilt of her neck to one side to indicate it being snapped. Thank fuck I was at Damian's. I feel sick with relief at my lucky escape and try to concentrate on what Sadie is saying.

… He must've got bored and hungry because he stormed in and hauled Elliott out of bed. He plunged his fangs into his neck, tasted his blood, and muttered, 'How intriguing.' I took the chance to jump on him, but he threw me on the floor. Elliott was yelling for me to save him. But Alexander compelled me to freeze in place, so I couldn't do anything. He dragged him off.

Me: *I just bumped into Alexander driving down Leith Walk. Elliott must've been in the back seat of his car.*

Sadie moans and rocks when she hears that.

If you'd both done your duties like I asked you to, we wouldn't be in this position. Not only is he our only source of blood, Elliott is my—

Sadie cuts off abruptly with an anguished look.

Me: *I'm really sorry.*

Hester: No, *it's my fault, Floss. I take full responsibility. I've been distracted lately. For different reasons ...*

Sadie (silently screaming at us): *I'm going to stake you both if he dies!*

I glance at Hester. *Holy shit.*

Hester: *We have to get him back. But exactly how we're going to manage that, I have no idea.*

Distressed and fearing for my life on two counts now, I sit back on my heels and discover Damian has escaped Hester's clutches and rounded the bed. He's staring bug-eyed at blood-soaked, wailing Sadie.

'What the hell is going on? Where's Elliott?'

'I take it back, Dr Rhodes. It *is* major.' I attempt to sound unconcerned but fail miserably. 'In fact, the situation has just been elevated to a monumental disaster.'

TO BE CONTINUED ...

Find out what happens next in Book 2
Enthralled By You – Sadie and Elliott's story –
featuring a slow burn spicy romance,
triple timeline and a vampire road trip to
the Scottish Highlands!

Books by Angela

FANGED AND FLIRTY SERIES

Flossed In Love

MISS AUSTEN SERIES

Trusting Miss Austen
Visiting Miss Austen
Amusing Miss Austen

STANDALONES

POX
Brontë Lovers
The Holly Project
You Had Me at Ice Cream
I'll Meet You in Florence
The House of Dating Disasters
My Double Life
Travel & Mayhem

COLLECTIONS

3 Book Rom-Com Collection

All books available on Amazon and Kindle Unlimited

Acknowledgements

Thank you for reading *Flossed In Love*, I hope you enjoyed it as much as I did writing it! If so, I'd be thrilled if you left a review or star rating on Amazon and/or Goodreads.

I'm so grateful for having a team of people to help me on the publishing journey. Thank you to my beta readers—Katharen Martin, Joanna Woollcombe-Gosson, Esther Kiburi, Jessica Taylor, Alicia Hastings, Emily Ladner, Mandy Bartmess (and my partner Chris Lambert)—for their insights and encouraging comments. Big thanks also to my diligent copy editor, Peachy Yap, and to My Lan Khuc Valle for her gorgeous cover art!

Check out the *Flossed In Love* Spotify playlist at

➜ angelapearse.pub/book-spotify-playlists

Join my mailing list for new releases,
offers, and bookish news!

➜ angelapearse.pub

About the Author

ANGELA PEARSE writes contemporary, historical and paranormal romances. Known for her quirky humour, Angela's books are often described as "page-turners", ranging from lighthearted escapades to darker satire.

A freelance editor with an MA in English, Angela is originally from New Zealand but now calls Edinburgh home, finding endless inspiration in its rich history and atmospheric streets. Visit angelapearse.pub for more information or to join her mailing list.